Two horses backed from the trailer as one. The mare curved around the foal with such tenderness, Sam could barely see him.

"Hotspot looks wonderful," Sam said, recalling what she'd heard of the foal's difficult birth and the mare's anxiety afterward. "But she sure doesn't want me to see—"

Sam broke off, hoping Ryan would supply the colt's name.

"Shy Boots," Ryan announced.

It suited him, Sam thought. Gangly and timid, the colt ducked his head, then peered up at Sam through impossibly long eyelashes.

"Ryan, he's darling."

"He'd rather be called 'magnificent,'" Ryan said. "But I suppose that will come with time."

Read all the books about the

Phantom Stallion

Phantom Stallion

∽15∽
Kidnapped Colt

TERRI FARLEY

AVON BOOKS

An Imprint of HarperCollinsPublishers

Library of Congress Catalog Card Number:
2004095710
ISBN 0-06-058316-9

First Avon edition, 2005

AVON TRADEMARK REG. U.S. PAT. OFF. AND IN OTHER COUNTRIES,
MARCA REGISTRADA, HECHO EN U.S.A.

❖

Visit us on the World Wide Web!
www.harperchildrens.com

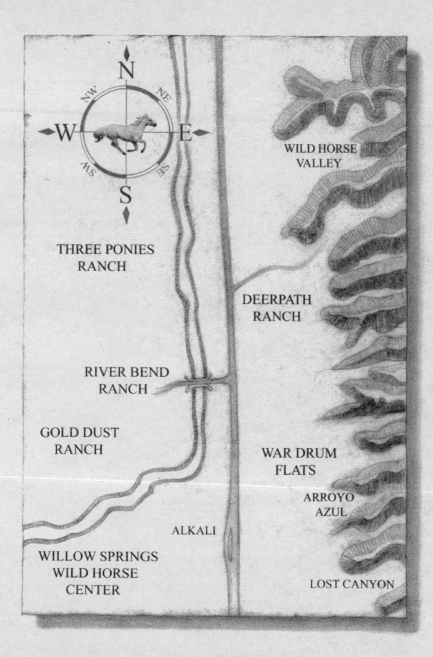

Chapter One ♌

*A*n albino mustang with crystal-blue eyes watched the ranch house. Samantha Forster watched back, holding the curtain aside so she could peer through the window in the kitchen door.

Even though the sun hadn't yet risen, a lot was going on at River Bend Ranch. Two cowboys had ridden out to check the stock. The foreman hammered a loose hinge on the barn door. Dad was tossing hay into the pasture and all the saddle horses—except Popcorn—jostled each other as they ate.

How did Popcorn know she was coming? And why did the captive mustang care?

A cold nose bumped Sam's palm, then Blaze yapped like a dog half his size.

"I know how to open the door," Sam told the border collie as he tried the movement again, lifting her hand toward the doorknob.

Sam stepped outside. Blaze knocked against her knee as he rocketed into the morning, but Sam stood still, rubbing warmth into her arms. Mornings started off bright and cold in Nevada's high desert country.

July sunlight, yellow as lemonade, shone over River Bend Ranch, while frost still sparkled on the fence around the ten-acre pasture. It wouldn't last long. Blue morning glory flowers vining up the chicken wire surrounding Gram's garden were halfway open.

It would be eighty degrees by noon.

Sam walked toward the ten-acre pasture where Popcorn waited. Her sneakers were quiet, but Ace and Strawberry noticed her approach and raised their heads, hay dropping from their lips.

Popcorn snorted, then tensed, forgetting all about Sam as an orange monarch butterfly landed on his nose.

The gelding's blue eyes crossed for an instant, trying to focus on the butterfly. As its wings spread, Popcorn shook his head, lashed out his hind legs, and launched into a gallop.

"I know you're just terrified of that tiny butterfly," Sam called after him.

Popcorn was tall for a mustang and his sturdy

build hinted at draft blood. His startled retreat wasn't due to fear, but high spirits.

Blaze rushed barking along the fence. Hooves thudded as other horses joined the morning run. Their glossy backs glinted bay, sorrel, and roan. Manes of black and tawny brown flew and their nostrils widened as they rejoiced in the scent of hoof-crushed grass.

This joyful stampede happened every morning, but it thrilled Sam every time.

"You ready?" Dallas, the ranch foreman called from the barn doorway.

"Just about."

Sam knew it was time to get busy. Today, she'd start training her month-old black filly, Tempest, to lead.

Before she took a single step toward Dallas, who was waiting to help, Gram called from the porch.

"Jen's on the phone. Do you have time to talk before you get started?"

Weird, Sam thought.

Last night when she'd talked with her best friend, Jen had moaned over the huge number of chores she had to finish before she was allowed to ride over to spend the week at River Bend Ranch.

It would be worth it, though. Not only would Jen be a new counselor for HARP, the Horse and Rider Protection program, but it was the week of the Fourth of July.

A parade, carnival, and other festivities were planned. They couldn't have picked a better time for a weeklong sleepover.

Since Jen's parents were leaving on a rare holiday away from the ranch, they were monitoring Jen's every move, making sure she finished her chores before they let her escape.

If Jen had made time for a phone call, it must be important.

"Sure," Sam said to Gram. Gesturing to Dallas, she added, "I'll be right back."

Inside, Sam took the telephone receiver, noticing a sticky spot from the oatmeal cookie dough Gram was mixing.

"Hello?" Sam said.

"How would you feel about a playdate?" Jen asked.

"A playdate?" Sam asked. She pictured her best friend's intelligent face and owlish eyes as she tried to make sense of the question. "Aren't we a little old for playdates?"

"Sure," Jen said, then she drew a breath so deep, Sam heard it. "But this isn't for us. Ryan wants his colt to come play with Tempest."

"Wow," Sam said. As she twirled in excitement, the phone cord wrapped around her. "That is so cool."

Ryan Slocum's colt was one day older than Tempest. On the open range, young horses raced around and learned how to be herd members by playing with other foals.

"That's perfect!" Then, as she disentangled herself from the cord, Sam's mind collided with a complication. Ryan's father, Linc Slocum. "Is it okay with his dad?"

Linc Slocum was the richest man in northern Nevada. No one knew exactly how he'd gotten so wealthy. Most folks were too neighborly to pry, but the wild schemes he'd pulled since he'd bought Gold Dust Ranch proved Linc Slocum didn't mind skirting the law.

"I'm not exactly sure Ryan's told his dad," Jen said. "Ryan said something about his father driving to Winnemucca to look at a custom-made saddle."

That figures, Sam thought.

Linc Slocum dreamed of being a real cowboy and thought he could buy the trappings to make people think he was one.

Ryan's colt was the offspring of one of those "trappings."

To Linc, Apache Hotspot, a blue-blooded Appaloosa mare, had looked like the perfect Western horse. He'd spent thousands of dollars on her and he'd planned to begin an Appaloosa breeding program. He'd been furious when Hotspot escaped, then turned up in foal to Diablo, a fierce blue roan stallion noted for his hammerhead.

Sam hadn't yet seen the foal, but she'd heard Linc

hated the colt as much as Ryan loved it.

"Sam, there's just one thing," Jen said, hesitantly.

Sam waited, stepping aside so Gram could get to the kitchen counter and check a crock that held rising bread dough.

"What is it?" Sam asked.

"I'll let Ryan tell you," Jen said. "Or beg you, I guess. It's kind of a big favor."

"Really?" Sam asked. "Ryan can buy anything he wants. What kind of favor could he need from me?"

"You have to say yes, Sam," Jen insisted. "He wouldn't ask if it wasn't important."

"Can't you do it?" Sam asked. Jen's persistent voice made her uneasy.

"Not this time."

"You can do anything I can. And more." *Besides, you're the one with the crush on him*, Sam thought, but she said, "And you're the one he likes."

"I can't give him the permission he needs to do this," Jen said with forced patience. "But you can."

Sam didn't like the sound of that.

"Now you've got me really worried," Sam said.

Despite his money and good looks, Ryan didn't have much backbone. Weakness could get you in big trouble here, where life hadn't left the frontier days totally behind.

Looking up, Sam wished she'd kept that last sentence to herself. Judging by Gram's frown as she stirred her cookie dough, she'd heard.

"Tell him to come on over, and we'll see," Sam told Jen, then she glanced at the kitchen clock. "I've got to go. Dallas is waiting for me."

"You're a pal," Jen said, sighing. "I'll be over as soon as I can."

"Hurry," Sam encouraged her. Then, so that Jen could do just that, Sam said good-bye.

"What's that all about?" Gram asked.

"Ryan's going to bring his colt over to play with Tempest."

"How nice," Gram said. She raised one eyebrow, as if she expected an explanation of what she'd over-heard.

Sam edged toward the door, even though she doubted Gram would let her escape.

She only had three steps left to go, then two, when Gram asked, "Sam, what has you worried?"

"I'm not sure," Sam said honestly.

Jen had sounded nervous. That was not like her.

And if Ryan planned to "beg" her to do something before his dad returned, his favor must be something sneaky.

Gram would not approve.

"I want plenty of time to work with Tempest before the HARP girls get here," Sam admitted. "I think the first day is the most important."

Gram studied Sam as if she might draw out another reason.

"I wonder if you're also just a little bit worried

Ryan's colt will be like his sire," Gram suggested.

"Diablo was fierce," Sam admitted. The chaos of fighting stallions, with the biting, kicking, and screaming neighs of superiority, came back to her. "But this is just a baby. Besides," Sam paused, smiling as she reduced the stallions' battle to a schoolyard boast, "Tempest's daddy beat his daddy."

Gram laughed, then fluttered a hand toward the door.

"Dallas isn't good at waiting, so you'd best get along out there. I won't expect to see you 'til lunchtime."

Sam kissed Gram's cheek, then bolted out the door toward the barn, trying to make up for lost time by running.

Sam heard Tempest's tiny hooves galloping around the barn corral. As she drew closer, Sam heard the filly huff with exertion.

"Don't know that you'll ever be able to use her with those HARP kids," Dallas said as Sam opened the gate to the barn corral and eased inside.

Instantly, Sam could tell Dallas wasn't talking about Tempest.

Dallas held a lead rope clipped to Dark Sunshine's halter. Dallas had been foreman on River Bend Ranch for as long as Sam could remember. The only time she'd seen his gray hair this disheveled was during last summer's barn fire.

Dark Sunshine's mane was just as untidy.

Torrents of black hair stood up on her crest and tangled against her brown-gold neck. The mare glared past her forelock with accusing eyes.

"What happened?" Sam asked.

"Had us a little set-to," Dallas explained, with a glance toward Tempest.

The filly's slender legs slowed to a trot. Her head swung from side to side, considering her mother, Sam, then her mother again.

"I thought it might be a good idea to keep the mare inside the barn," Dallas continued. "That way the filly could concentrate on her lesson. But the buckskin had a different opinion."

"Sorry," Sam said.

"Didn't seem like a good day to insist," Dallas said.

Sam nodded in agreement. In a few hours, the HARP girls would arrive. And then there was Ryan, but she wouldn't tell Dallas about that until she had to.

There was a good chance she and Dallas were already destined for a day of butting heads. They'd never agreed about handling horses. Though he was kind, he believed in telling horses what to do. Sam liked to try asking first.

"Mare doesn't know how to be tame," Dallas pointed out, as he handed Tempest's halter and lead rope to Sam.

Like most cowboys, Dallas only said a tenth of what he was thinking.

Did he mean Dark Sunshine never should have been captured? Sam wondered. Or that she should have been carrying a saddle and rider by now?

Sam studied Dallas's sun-lined face, hoping he'd go on.

"Once the filly's weaned, you'll want to see to that," Dallas said.

Sam's heart zigzagged in fear or excitement. She couldn't tell which as she answered, "I will."

Bidding for Sam's attention, Tempest skittered up, within reach, and stopped.

Blue-black in the sunlight, the filly dipped her head, then lifted it, waiting for the sound of her secret name. But Dallas stood too close.

"Makes more sense to wean a foal before breaking it to lead," Dallas said. He skimmed a callused hand along Dark Sunshine's neck, rewarding her for staying calm.

"Tempest doesn't mind the halter," Sam said.

"She's still kinda young," Dallas said.

Dallas had already had a half century of horse experience on the day Sam had been born. She respected that. He was River Bend's foreman, too. Only Gram and Dad had more say-so in how the ranch was run.

If she hadn't been present for Tempest's birth, if she hadn't spent hours bonding with the filly, Sam would have accepted Dallas's advice. But she knew Tempest. This time Dallas was wrong.

Since she couldn't argue with him, Sam decided she'd let Dallas see for himself how Tempest accepted the halter.

"Hey, baby girl," Sam crooned as she slipped the noseband over Tempest's muzzle, lifted the halter into place, and lay the thin leather strap behind the filly's flicking black ears. Finally, Sam fastened the buckle.

Tempest didn't protest. She only stamped one tiny hoof, urging Sam to rub behind her ears as she always did after the buckle was fastened.

Sam smiled. She was never quick enough to satisfy the filly.

"It's your call," Dallas said, though his tone insisted she was making a mistake trying to teach such a youngster to lead.

"She trusts me," Sam explained.

Tempest closed her eyes and leaned harder into the fingers kneading behind her ears.

"Trust'll mean nothin' if she's scared. When you snap on that lead rope, she'll run to her mama."

Sam looked Tempest over carefully. She didn't look like she was poised to make a dash for her mother. She looked drowsy.

"If you don't take Sunny into the barn, maybe Tempest won't run after her."

"Horses are prey animals," Dallas insisted. "Something happens that filly don't understand, and it's natural she'll run from it. Just be ready, is all I'm sayin'."

Still rubbing Tempest's velvety head, Sam imagined Tempest bolting, then hitting the end of the rope with all her energy. She could fall. That would be a bad introduction to the world of ropes and reins.

"What if we start inside the stall?" Sam asked.

"Good idea," Dallas said.

Amazed at Dallas's approval, Sam gave a quick laugh, but the old foreman was already leading Dark Sunshine to the barn.

The mare walked with him, but her ears flicked back, then sideways.

"It's okay, girl," Sam assured the buckskin mare.

Sunny's golden-brown head swung to consider Sam. Then she kept walking. The mare wasn't sure two people belonged inside the stall she shared with her foal, but she didn't fight the pull of the lead.

Neither did Tempest. When Sam snapped the soft cotton rope onto Tempest's halter, the filly didn't seem to notice.

"All right," Sam crowed quietly.

For about ten minutes, Dallas moved Dark Sunshine from side to side, then from one end to the other, of her box stall. Sam let Tempest do the same.

Piece of cake, Sam was thinking, when Dallas spoke up.

"It'll be a whole other thing when you try to lead her," Dallas warned. "But let's try it."

Walking with bowlegged stiffness, Dallas led Dark Sunshine out of the stall and back into the corral. Tempest followed, with only an annoyed look for the tension on the rope as Sam hurried to keep up.

"You watch her every second," Dallas said. "She's little enough you can hold her if you're not surprised."

"Got it," Sam agreed. Experience had taught her that horses took advantage of humans who didn't pay attention.

Crab-stepping along, Sam kept up with Dallas and Dark Sunshine and still watched Tempest.

"Makin' a good start," Dallas said.

Sam tried not to feel smug, but maybe she'd convinced Dallas that kindness could win over wildness.

Not too bad for a girl who spent two years off the ranch and in the city, Sam congratulated herself.

Suddenly Tempest's ears tensed and pointed.

Sam heard the rumble, too. An unfamiliar vehicle was crossing the River Bend bridge.

Dark Sunshine shied and snorted.

"No ya don't." Dallas pronounced the words with calm determination.

Then he coiled the lead rope before taking long strides that forced the buckskin to keep up.

It's okay, Sam thought, but Tempest squealed. She protested her desertion, though her mother moved just steps ahead. The filly dashed forward and the lead was already slipping through Sam's fingers when her hands closed tight.

Just then, Tempest reached the end of the rope.

The sudden tension spun her around to face Sam.

"I'm sorry, baby, I'm sorry," Sam soothed.

"Don't be," Dallas corrected. "You're only showing her what you want."

Tempest reared. Ears flattened and eyes narrowed, she reminded Sam she was a mustang.

Front hooves pawing the air, the filly might have been saying, *Do you know who my father is?*

But suddenly the foal faltered. Off balance, she fell forward and Sam felt a flash of pain.

As Tempest managed to get all four hooves beneath her, Sam touched her cheek. It felt hot where Tempest's right hoof had struck.

It hurt. A lot. Enough to make her cry, usually, but right now she had something to prove and crying wouldn't help.

Sam couldn't help glancing toward Dallas.

"You okay?" He sounded worried.

As soon as she nodded, Dallas turned angry.

"You tried bein' gentle, but her mustang blood is boilin'. If you don't show her who's boss, you'll wreck her."

Chapter Two ❧

"I won't wreck her," Sam insisted.

She wanted to face Dallas. And she wanted to see who'd driven over the bridge and into the ranch yard, but Sam didn't take her eyes off Tempest.

"You're a good, sweet girl," Sam murmured.

The black filly listened and changed tactics. Her tantrum turned into determined sidestepping toward her mother.

"You want to go see your mama?" Sam asked. From across the pen, she heard Dark Sunshine pawing. "Then we have to walk there together."

Holding her breath, Sam gripped the rope and walked toward the mare.

This time, it was Sam who hit the end of the rope

with a jerk. Tempest's weight acted like an anchor. The filly refused to be led anywhere.

Tempest whinnied and shook her head. She reared again, hooves pawing at the halter.

"Oh, baby," Sam sighed.

Settling back on all fours, the filly snorted hard. She did it three times, head lowered, as if she could sneeze the halter off.

Then she glanced away.

Sam didn't turn to follow the filly's eyes. From the corner of her eye, though, Sam saw a champagne-colored Jeep Cherokee pulling a matching horse trailer.

Ryan was here.

"You got company," Dallas said.

"I know," Sam said.

The Jeep's door opened, then shut.

"You done for the day?" Dallas's question sounded like a dare.

"No," Sam snapped back.

Of course she was curious about Ryan's favor, and eager to see his colt, but she'd already messed up the beginning of Tempest's training. Sam would not stop now.

Feeling Sam's distraction, Tempest sidestepped toward her mother.

"I'm going with you," Sam told the filly. "And you're going to keep looking at me until you figure out what's going on."

As clearly as if she'd said, "No, I'm not," Tempest turned around.

"Put a loop around her hindquarters and tug her along," Dallas said.

Sam shook her head.

"If you did, she couldn't pull that on you," Dallas chuckled, amused that Sam found herself staring at Tempest's tail instead of watching the filly's face.

"I know." Sam tried to sound patient.

"And your friend wouldn't —"

"He can wait!" Sam interrupted.

"Of course," Ryan's voice, with its British accent, sounded cool and so polite, Sam felt her face heat with a blush.

But Ryan was a horseman. Surely he'd understand.

She refused to force the filly. Popcorn, Penny, and Dark Sunshine were all proof that forcing mustangs, instead of teaching them, created problems.

Holding the rope snug, but not pulling, Sam worked her way around so that she could see Tempest's face again.

The filly blew through her lips. Then, maybe by accident, she took a step forward.

"Good girl." Sam sang the words. Since she couldn't reward the filly with her secret name, Sam allowed a little slack in the rope.

That captured Tempest's full attention. Brown

eyes glistening, the little black mustang studied Sam as if she were trying to read her mind.

Give me one teeny, tiny sign you know what I'm asking you for, and we're done, Sam thought.

The filly kept staring.

Even though Dark Sunshine nickered, Tempest's eyes stayed on Sam's.

Slowly and deliberately, Tempest lifted a front hoof and placed it ahead of the others. She rocked forward, testing. Her gleaming black head tilted to one side.

It wasn't quite a step, but Tempest had created her own slack in the rope, and that was a good start.

"You got it." Sam came down the rope to touch Tempest's back.

The filly lifted her head, then ducked it, looking like a black swan as she asked for the sound of her secret name. This time, Sam moved close enough to answer. Closing her eyes, Sam stroked the filly's neck in long, smooth movements, then whispered, "Xanadu."

She'd first heard the word in a mystical poem read to the class by her English teacher. Instantly, Sam had heard how it echoed the Phantom's secret name.

Even when she'd discovered that Xanadu only sounded like it began with a Z, like Zanzibar, it had remained in her mind as the perfect secret name for the Phantom's foal with Dark Sunshine.

"Xanadu," Sam whispered once more, and the

filly relaxed against her.

Let Dallas and Ryan think she spoke nonsense to the filly. This was magic only she and Tempest knew.

Sam slipped off Tempest's halter. She wouldn't take a chance that Tempest would rear and paw at it again. If she caught a hoof through the cheek strap, she could fall and break one of her slender legs.

Before Sam could move away and tell the filly she was free, Tempest began sniffing her sleeve.

"It's me," Sam told her. "I'm the one asking you to understand all this crazy stuff."

Tempest gave a huff of milky breath, then trotted off to her mother, just as Dallas set the mare loose.

As Sam turned toward Dallas, her legs felt soft as noodles. She wasn't sure they'd hold her up.

Dallas stared at her cheek.

"What?" Sam said, hands on hips. But she sounded so rude, she tried to amend her snappish question. "I'll put ice on it later, okay?"

"Fine," Dallas said, then turned to go.

"Wait. Dallas? Thanks for helping me. I'm sorry—"

He gave a "go on" gesture.

"I just want to try training her the way I did Blackie," Sam said.

Was Dallas looking pointedly toward the range, indicating her technique had resulted in losing Blackie? After all, he had escaped to become the powerful stallion known as the Phantom. No. Sam realized Dallas was focused on the sounds coming from the horse trailer.

"Ryan brought his colt over to play with Tempest," Sam explained. "Do you think that'd be all right?"

Dallas nodded slowly. "If you keep the mares quiet, I don't see what it can hurt."

"Thanks," Sam said on a sigh, and then she turned to Ryan.

Linc Slocum's son was as smooth and reserved as his father was lumpy and loud.

Dressed in a tan polo shirt and jeans, Ryan had sleek coffee-colored hair that he wore a little long. He looked European, rich and, right now, relieved.

"Did Jennifer tell you what I had in mind?" Ryan asked.

"About the colts," Sam said.

"Ah." He sounded disappointed, but just for a second. Had he expected Jen to ask the favor for him? Apparently not, because Ryan's eyes brightened as he asked, "Would you like a look at him, then?"

Sam guessed her grin was answer enough, because Ryan moved to open the back of the trailer.

The seconds it took Ryan to work the trailer latch free cranked up Sam's eagerness until she wanted to jump in and help.

Would the colt be an Appaloosa like his sweet-tempered mother or a stocky, heavy-headed animal like his sire?

The thick-maned stallion had been named Diablo by his owner, Rosa Perez. That was Spanish for "devil," but Rosa had claimed the stallion was "mild as a dove" with her.

Two horses backed from the trailer as one. The mare curved around the foal with such tenderness, Sam could barely see him.

She had forgotten Apache Hotspot was so beautiful. The young mare showed the best of her Thoroughbred and Appaloosa heritage. Her cocoa-brown head, neck, mane, and front legs flowed into a snow-white body sprinkled with brown.

"Hotspot looks wonderful," Sam said, recalling what she'd heard of the foal's difficult birth and the mare's anxiety afterward. "But she sure doesn't want me to see —"

Sam broke off, hoping Ryan would supply the colt's name.

"Shy Boots," Ryan announced.

It suited him, Sam thought, as Hotspot danced restlessly aside.

Gangly and timid, the colt ducked his head, then peered up at Sam through impossibly long eyelashes.

"Ohhh." Sam felt an instant tug at her heart.

Cocoa-brown like his dam, Shy Boots had a perfect white blanket over his hips. It was marked with spatters that looked like chocolate snowflakes. Pure white stockings reached from his faintly striped hooves to his knees.

"Ryan, he's darling."

"He'd rather be called 'magnificent,'" Ryan said. "But I suppose that will come with time."

Sam laughed. Sophisticated Ryan was actually speaking for his horse. Sam did it all the time, but this was the first time she'd heard it from him.

A squeaking snort came from the barn corral. Sam turned to see Tempest pressing against the fence, watching Shy Boots.

"She wants to play with him," Sam said.

"Then we won't keep the lady waiting," Ryan said.

He led Hotspot toward the corral, and Sam opened the gate. Shy Boots stayed so close to his mother, their burnished coats seemed to merge.

Until he saw Tempest.

Then, the colt frisked a few brave steps away.

Dark Sunshine flattened her ears, warning the newcomers from across the pen.

"Dallas said we should keep hold of the mares, at least 'til we see how they do together," Sam said.

"Very well," Ryan said.

The foals wasted no time inspecting each other.

Black muzzle touched brown before two exploring nickers erupted. Tempest made loud snuffling noises as she sniffed the colt's face. Shy Boots flicked his ears back and rolled his eyes. Tempest's ears sagged to each side, showing the colt she meant no harm by her curiosity.

Both foals raised their heads. Each tried to reach higher, until Shy Boots reared and Tempest snapped her teeth at his front legs.

Sam glanced at Dark Sunshine, but the mare had fallen to grazing. That must mean she wasn't worried.

As they reached some equine agreement, both foals' tiny brushlike tails flicked up and they burst into a run. Circling the corral, Tempest chased Shy Boots, nipping at his tail. Shy Boots zigzagged past his mother, nearly rammed Dark Sunshine, then wheeled to confront Tempest. They were off again, this time with Tempest in retreat.

Their joy was contagious. Across the ranch yard, the saddle herd began galloping around the ten-acre pasture, too.

"Last year your dad said Hotspot's foal might be 'fast as a caged squirrel,'" Sam told Ryan.

"He does manage those long legs rather well." Ryan sounded like a parent trying to be modest.

Ryan looked so proud and so fond of Shy Boots, she decided not to mention that Linc had also said she could have the foal.

Something in Shy Boots cut through Ryan's cold reserve and made him happy. She wouldn't think of holding Linc to his offer.

The foals returned to their mothers and nursed so briefly, it seemed they were checking in, rather than seeking meals.

Dark Sunshine rested her chin on Tempest's

back. Hotspot grazed and Shy Boots imitated her, spreading his front legs wide as he tried to nibble the sparse grass.

"Is he eating solid food already?" Sam asked.

"Trying," Ryan said. "Each day he chews more and nurses less."

Dark Sunshine was more watchful of Tempest than Hotspot was of Shy Boots. As Sam and Ryan eased out of the pen, Sam saw Dallas and mentioned the difference between the two mares.

"That's the way of it," Dallas said. "While they're little, filly foals are closer to their mamas. Once they're yearlings, though, the moms show more attachment to the colts."

Sam mulled that over, trying to make sense of it. Since young mares and young stallions were both driven from the herds by their sires, what were the mares thinking?

Tired out, Shy Boots flung himself down for a nap beside his grazing mother. As his tiny brown head scrubbed back and forth in the grass, trying to find a comfortable position, Sam decided his delicate bone structure showed no sign of his hammerhead father.

Tempest watched her playmate doze, but when she turned to bite the area above her tail, scratching an itch, she did it loudly. Then she used a hind hoof to scratch behind her ear. Fighting for balance, Tempest squealed, then looked at Shy Boots to see if he'd noticed.

The colt's long eyelashes stayed closed.

"She's doing everything she can to get his attention," Sam said as Tempest bolted into another lap around the corral. "I wish he and Hotspot could stay."

"So do I." Ryan spoke up quickly, as if Sam's words were the go-ahead he'd needed. "That's what I intended to ask of you."

So this was why Jen had said she couldn't give Ryan the permission he needed. Sam swallowed hard. There was no way in the universe Dad would allow more horses at the ranch.

"Then, as I drove over here," Ryan went on, "I realized my father would find them at River Bend."

"Find them?" Sam asked.

Ryan drew a breath. His explanation was probably going to be a long one.

"A few days ago, my father had Hotspot trailered over to Sterling Stables to be bred to Cloud Cap, a stallion of *good* bloodlines," Ryan began.

Sam nodded.

"Shy Boots went along, since he's still nursing," Ryan said. "And, according to everyone watching, that's why, when Cloud Cap was loosed to Hotspot, she attacked him. She thought she needed to protect Shy Boots from the stallion."

She might have been right, Sam thought. In mustang herds, stallions sometimes killed foals that weren't their own.

"When Mr. Sterling opened the gate, Cloud Cap didn't have to be coaxed away from Hotspot. He fled." Ryan's shoulders lifted in a slight shrug. "Mr. Sterling suggested a second try after Shy Boots was weaned. He was polite about it, saying it happened now and then, but when my father returned home, he condemned Boots as a mongrel that had ruined everything."

"You can't let him think that way," Sam warned Ryan. She'd seen Linc Slocum's cruelty. The Phantom wore a scar from it.

"I did my best," Ryan said. "I reminded him of Hotspot's bloodlines and Diablo's stamina. Eventually, he calmed down. He agreed—at least I thought he had—to merely wean Boots early."

"He's only a few weeks old," Sam protested.

"I know. I'm afraid he'll be perpetually timid." Ryan stared away from the corral, past River Bend's bridge. "Hotspot is his only family. Take him away too young and he'll have no one but me." Ryan gave a short, mocking laugh. "And I'm the last one who could teach him what it means to be a Western horse."

"Ryan . . ." Sam began, but Ryan motioned her to wait.

"All the same, I agreed to early weaning, because it seemed the safest route."

Safest? Sam didn't like the sound of that.

"This morning, I was supposed to take Hotspot

back to Sterling Stables without Boots."

Ryan cleared his throat, then he gripped both of Sam's shoulders.

She would have twisted away if he hadn't looked down into her eyes with desperation.

"This morning, before I left, my father was on the telephone telling someone that the easiest way to 'wean' Boots was to *cull* him."

"What did he mean by that?" Sam asked, but her heart was already plummeting.

Linc Slocum had scarred the Phantom's neck and caused much of the stallion's dislike for humans. What would he do to a "mongrel" foal like Shy Boots?

"He wants to have Boots destroyed."

Horror slashed through Sam's imagination. She thought of bullets, syringes full of poison. . . . But when her eyes settled on Shy Boots, she realized it wouldn't take much to end his new life.

"Please," Ryan said, when Sam stayed silent. "Help me hide them where my father won't think to look. I wouldn't ask, Samantha, but you're my only hope."

Chapter Three ❧

 *H*iding horses wasn't the same as stealing them, but would her dad see the difference? Sam didn't think so.

"Won't that just delay the problem?" she asked Ryan.

"I think not," Ryan said with sudden confidence. "For two reasons. First, the time for breeding Hotspot will be past. Second, my father is certain to lose interest." Ryan's lips twisted into a mocking smile. "You may have noticed Father's passion for projects is rather short-lived."

Ryan was right.

"It might work," Sam agreed. "But you don't need me—"

"Ah, but I do. I can't find the box canyon you and Jennifer discovered. Not alone."

"I don't know," Sam said, stalling.

"She told me it has shade and water, everything they'd need to wait this out."

"Yeah," Sam said. She and Jen *had* found a shady box canyon big enough to hold a few cattle, and it was silly to feel jealous over Jen telling him about it. "It's up near High Grass Canyon, halfway to Cowkiller Caldera, but . . ."

Ryan forced the fingers of one hand through his dark hair, looking worried. He loved his horses and she wanted to help him, but this felt wrong.

"Ryan, I know the canyon sounds like a solution, but I'm not sure it's safe. There are predators up there. Cougars, coyotes —" Sam stopped, shaking her head. Did Jen really think this was a good idea? "And it's right on the edge of the Phantom's territory."

"Oh, not that fable again," Ryan said.

Fine, Sam thought. She'd let Ryan believe her silver stallion was imaginary. The Phantom would be safer that way.

Suddenly Ryan fixed Sam with a stare.

"You do know there's blood on your face," he said.

"It doesn't hurt," Sam snapped.

She glared at Ryan. Was he grossed out by a spot of blood? Did he think embarrassing her would make her more likely to go along?

"I'm sorry," Ryan said, at last. "I don't know why

I brought that up. I'm awfully attached to Boots and my feelings are in a tangle."

He continued, "You're right, of course, that stallions gather mares. But how can I listen to prattle about magical horses when Boots's life is at stake?"

"I never said he was magical," Sam insisted. "But he's strong. If he or any wild stallion wanted to add Hotspot to his herd, no fence would stop him."

Sam pictured New Moon, the Phantom's pure black son, and Yellow Tail, a wild chestnut stallion. Either horse could leap a fence, then use nips and neighs to drive Hotspot and Shy Boots away.

"It happened to her once before," Sam reminded Ryan. "Diablo herded her right off Gold Dust Ranch."

"You may be right," Ryan conceded.

I am right, Sam thought, but Ryan had grown up in England. Her descriptions of wild horses and mountain lions probably sounded like Wild West fantasies to him.

"I agree there's an element of danger in my plan," Ryan admitted, "but it's worth the risk. And I'll take full responsibility."

"Promise?" Sam asked.

"You have my word on it," Ryan said. "All you have to do is lead me there."

As Sam watched, Tempest walked close enough to the sleeping Shy Boots to nibble his fluffy mane.

C'mon, wake up, she seemed to say, but she was gentle.

"All right," Sam said at last. "I'll do it if my father agrees. He and Brynna should be back in a couple hours."

Agitated, Ryan looked at his silver watch as if he had an appointment to keep.

"We don't have a couple of hours," Ryan insisted.

"What's the difference, if—"

"It's only three hours from here to Winnemucca and my father's a fast driver. If he gets back, wonders why I'm taking so long delivering Hotspot, and notices Boots is gone, the entire effort of bringing them to you is wasted. Boots will be destroyed anyway. The only difference is, you will have thrown away a chance to save him."

"Me? That's not fair."

"Sam, do you think it's easy for me to beg for your help?" Ryan set his jaw.

His expression said he'd expected more of her, but Sam knew she was right. Blaming her wasn't fair.

Sam ran back through all the reasons why she shouldn't go along with Ryan. She crossed her arms and stared at the ground. If she looked at Shy Boots, she knew she'd weaken.

Because Linc was so cruel, she could ignore the feeling that she was almost stealing the horses.

But what about the cougars and coyotes?

Jen was a science whiz. If she thought the horses would be safe, maybe she was right.

Sam sighed and looked at her own watch.

"What about this," Ryan countered. "I'll just hide them there until morning."

"Predators hunt at dusk," Sam said.

No matter what Jen thought, Sam was afraid of cougars. She'd been the intended prey of one and the memory was never far away.

Her muscles tightened, as if she could feel the crash of the young cougar against her back. It hadn't been the cat's fault, but that moment had been the most frightening of her life.

Shy Boots wouldn't survive such an attack. Even if Hotspot fought for his life, she was a stable-bred horse and no match for a wild animal with slashing teeth and claws. Even mustang mares lost foals to hungry cougars.

"Help me do this now and I'll talk with Father as soon as he returns from Winnemucca. I'll make him understand, then bring the horses home before the sun goes down. If I fail, I'll stay overnight with them," Ryan promised.

"You will?" Sam asked, surprised.

She tried to meet his eyes, but Ryan looked down.

He really loved Hotspot and Shy Boots, Sam thought. He must be hiding tears.

"All right," Sam said. "But we have to hurry."

Minutes later, Hotspot and Boots had been reloaded into the trailer, Sam had gathered a staple gun and a roll of plastic fence, and she was giving thanks that she hadn't run into Dallas while she was gathering them. But she still had to face Gram. If she sneaked away without saying where she was going, she'd be grounded for life.

Since Gram was busy baking for the HARP girls' arrival, maybe she'd be too distracted to pay close attention. Hoping so, Sam started talking the minute she opened the kitchen door.

"Gram, I'm going to help Ryan—"

Gram blew a wisp of gray hair away from her eyes as she turned, holding a sheet of cookies she'd just taken from the oven.

"My word, what have you done to your cheek?"

Gram set the hot cookie sheet down with a clatter.

"It's nothing. In fact, I forgot all about it. I hurt it when I was working with Tempest," Sam admitted.

"Go wash your face. Then, bring me the hydrogen peroxide, some gauze, and"—Gram frowned in concentration, clearly judging the size of the cut—"a big Band-Aid should do it."

"Ryan needs me to—" Sam began.

"Ryan can wait. I don't want you getting some sort of infection." Gram reached for a spatula. "Besides, he'll forget his impatience when you bring him some cookies."

Without another protest, Sam did as Gram asked.

She turned on the water and was about to splash her face when she saw her image in the bathroom mirror. No wonder Dallas, Ryan, and Gram had all mentioned the injury.

"Yuck," she told her reflection.

Tempest's hoof had sliced an inch-long cut over her cheekbone. The spot was swollen and dusty. Blood had smeared all around it.

She gingerly dabbed water to tidy the wound. When it was pretty clean, she descended the stairs, not really looking forward to Gram's tending.

"Where are you two going?" Gram asked, after she'd squeezed a stinging fizz of peroxide over the cut, wiped it, and smoothed on a bandage.

"He wants me to show him how to get to High Grass Canyon," Sam explained, moving her cheek experimentally. It felt stiff, but it didn't hurt.

"You could draw him a map, but I'm sure that wouldn't be half as much fun," Gram mused. "Leave those things and I'll put them away," she said, waving toward the first aid supplies. "You just worry about hurrying home."

With that, Gram turned her attention back to baking.

One minute later, Sam was sitting in the front seat of Ryan's truck, watching him munch oatmeal cookies as the truck bumped over the bridge and onto the highway.

"I promised to be back before Brynna and Dad get here with the new HARP girls," Sam warned.

"You will be," Ryan vowed.

Sam was examining her puffy cheek in the truck's

rearview mirror, when Ryan leaned to one side and his image replaced hers.

At first she thought he was looking at himself, but his hopeful expression surprised her.

She turned toward him and saw his hand lift to wave.

The truck coming toward them was huge and yellow. She didn't recognize the driver as it passed by.

"Who's that?" she asked.

"Karl Mannix."

It took a minute for Sam to remember the name.

"The guy who sold your dad the deerhounds?" Sam asked. "Are you friends?"

Just last week, the Louisiana deerhounds had caused Dad's horse to fall with him. Not long after that, the hounds had cornered a mustang foal. Deer-hunting dogs were illegal in Nevada, but only the near disasters had convinced Linc to send them back where they belonged.

"No, we're not friends. Why would you think that? He just works for my father. He's supposed to be a cowboy," Ryan said dubiously, "but I heard Jed Kenworthy tell Mrs. Cole that 'this fella Karl' was supposed to be a cattle expert who raised black Angus." Ryan pronounced the name of the breed of cattle uncertainly. "Then Jed added that Mr. Mannix knew more about stocks and bonds than livestock."

Sam made an understanding noise.

She guessed she'd misinterpreted Ryan's expression. Even though he was new to Nevada, he understood that cowboying took skills most people didn't have.

Driving over the foothills between War Drum Flats and Arroyo Azul took no time at all in the truck, but the terrain began changing from alkali flats and sagebrush to pinion pine–covered slopes. Riding this wild country on horseback was easier than tackling it with a truck and trailer.

As they hit a washboard-rutted bit of road, Sam's cheek ached. She should have taken some aspirin to ward off the soreness.

"Hold on," Ryan warned, but Sam wasn't prepared for the swerve that slammed her against the passenger side door.

"Sorry. I was trying to miss that rut," he explained.

The road had narrowed to a rough trail.

When she and Jen had ridden here, the horses had stepped around the rain-sculpted washouts and small rock slides.

"We're getting close," she told Ryan.

"And a good thing. This is becoming somewhat tricky."

Ryan slowed the Jeep to a crawl. Still, hardened furrows of mud shook the vehicle, making her cheek twinge each time, but it was the worried shifting of hooves in the trailer behind them that made her want to stop.

"It's only another mile or so to the box canyon," Sam said, looking up the hillside. "Shall we lead them in?"

"Great idea," Ryan said.

Avoiding a boulder with a white scuff across its face, Ryan pulled the truck to the right side of the road, put on the emergency brake so the Jeep wouldn't roll backward down the steep hill, and turned the key to "off."

Unnerved by the bumpy ride, Hotspot backed out of the trailer at full speed, knocking Ryan aside before he reached her lead.

But Sam was quick enough to snag the leather strap.

"Got her," Sam said.

Hotspot danced in place, lifting her knees and flaring her nostrils. After a few breaths, she seemed reassured.

Ears flicking, the Appaloosa inspected her surroundings, oblivious to Shy Boots's anxious nickers.

The colt stayed in the trailer until Ryan walked inside, looped a soft rope around his neck, and led him out.

"He leads?" Sam said.

Ryan had simply looped the rope around the colt's neck. He'd used no halter, no knots even, and Boots had followed him like a pet poodle.

Recalling the bucking fuss Tempest had put up, Sam could hardly believe it.

"Yes, he leads quite nicely," Ryan boasted. When he let the rope slip free, Shy Boots bolted forward to nudge Hotspot with his chocolate-brown nose.

Quite nicely, Sam's mind mimicked, but she couldn't picture herself asking Ryan for training tips.

"She's not afraid." Ryan smoothed his hand over the mare's sleek neck. "In England, I rode a big dappled beast of a horse named Voyager. He took any jump I put him at. Apparently, though, he'd never been out of sight of stables and riding rings.

"On a lark, I decided to try him over a cross-country course. He wouldn't even begin. He simply froze up. All four legs went stiff at the sight of forest and rolling hills."

"You'd think he'd just want to run," Sam said.

When she rode Ace, one glimpse of the wide range made him fight the bit, eager to gallop. But as she waited for Ryan's response, he seemed more uneasy than Hotspot.

That probably made sense, considering the mare had run the open range once before.

The first time she'd seen Hotspot, Sam had been riding with Jake near War Drum Flats. They'd spotted an elegant horse van as its driver unloaded the Appaloosa before starting to fix a flat tire. They'd offered to help, and while Sam held the mare, the

Phantom had appeared.

The silver stallion hadn't been bold enough to gallop down and introduce himself. Instead, he'd played hide-and-seek from the foothills, while the fascinated mare watched.

"You lead Hotspot and I'll wrestle this," Ryan said, interrupting the memory. He hefted the roll of orange plastic fencing over one shoulder and gripped the staple gun in the other. Then he glanced back down the trail, toward the highway, as if he was worried he'd been followed.

As they trudged uphill, Sam wished she'd been wearing anything but sneakers. They'd been great for working with Tempest this morning, but the smooth soles slipped as she hurried to stay beside Hotspot.

Even so, she tried to stay alert for signs of wild horses. With luck, Shy Boots' troubled nickers wouldn't draw predators.

"We've got to make him stop that," she told Ryan.

"He's just an infant. What do you expect?" Ryan didn't sound concerned as he shifted the fencing to his other shoulder and kept walking.

"I'm not trying to be mean," Sam said. "But every animal around here will recognize the sound of a small animal in distress. He won't be safe."

Ryan's shoe slipped on a patch of skree. He fought for balance, managing not to drop the roll of fencing, but he sounded frustrated as he went on. "I trust he'll be weary when we reach our destination and he'll fall asleep."

Sam hoped Ryan was right, but she had no faith in his prediction. She had a bad feeling about this.

Secret or not, she planned to tell Dad the minute he got home.

Chapter Four ∽

Sweat burned Sam's eyes. She'd already pushed her shirt sleeves above her elbows and tugged her collar open. She couldn't do much else to keep cool.

We were idiots not to bring a canteen, she thought. *No, I'm the idiot,* she corrected herself.

Ryan had been living in England, not Nevada. She couldn't expect him to be prepared, or to realize that even if he saw water, he shouldn't drink it.

Last week the box canyon had held a pool of snowmelt water that had been fine for the cattle, and it would probably be all right for the horses, but she knew humans could get all kinds of yucky intestinal sicknesses from water that wasn't freeflowing. She'd have to be totally desperate to take a drink there.

Sam was beginning to wonder if the trick she'd read about, holding a pebble in your mouth and sucking on it, really calmed your thirst, when she spotted tan cottonwood leaves standing out against the sky just beyond an outcropping of rock.

And there was the fallen tree with a black lightning scar on its trunk. She and Jen had seen it last week, just before Linc and the deerhounds exploded onto the trail.

"We're almost there," Sam said, striding out with a spurt of energy.

Responding to Sam's voice and the scent of water, Hotspot surged ahead. Sam jogged to keep up.

The box canyon was perfect for the horses.

Ryan dropped the roll of plastic fencing and stood watching as Hotspot and Shy Boots sucked in long swallows of water from the pool.

Sam didn't join his contemplation. She started building the barrier across the mouth of the canyon. It had been easy when she and Jen worked together, but now she grappled with the fencing. Any minute Ryan should notice she needed help.

He didn't.

"This took two of us last time," Sam hinted, but Ryan gave no sign that he heard her.

Sam sniffed and felt a twinge along her cheekbone.

This'll look great to meet the HARP girls, she thought as the plastic fence tried to curl out of her grasp.

Maybe I'll even get a black eye.

Time was slipping away. She had to get back to River Bend before Dad and Brynna did.

"Hey, Ryan," Sam called. Her voice silenced the birds on the quiet hillside. "I could use some help here."

"Sorry," he said. Then, as she watched, he gave Shy Boots's neck a hug. "I'm just saying good-bye."

Just saying good-bye. Alarm tightened Sam's chest.

"Ryan, it's only going to be a few hours until you see them again." Sam waited as Ryan pushed a lock of dark hair back from his forehead. "Right?"

Ryan blushed.

Like most guys, he hid his feelings, covering his love for the horses by getting busy. He took the staple gun from Sam and held it at an awkward angle.

"Explain the way of this, if you please," Ryan said. "And we'll be out of here."

They were nearly finished.

Sam stood inside the fence, facing Ryan across it.

The horses dozed in the shade behind her. Sam held the last section of fencing taut while Ryan prepared to place the final staple.

Blinking against a dazzling sun, Sam looked past Ryan and spotted the Phantom.

He hadn't approached from the trail. His hooves hadn't disturbed a single pebble. Sam couldn't guess which instinct made her notice him, off to the left of the faint trail leading up to Cowkiller Caldera.

The stallion hid in a tangle of juniper. Its three tallest branches speared skyward like a trident. Neck high in the brush, he would have been invisible, if the sky had been overcast. But it wasn't.

Sunlight picked out dapples that shone like silver coins on the Phantom's pale coat.

His ropey white forelock all but hid his eyes. Still, Sam knew this stallion, the most magnificent horse in the world, was watching her.

The stallion lifted his head and all at once he was crowned with a nimbus of sunlight.

She felt, rather than saw, the tremor move along his throat as he uttered a silent greeting.

Zanzibar. Sam sent out his secret name.

The stallion's Arab-fine ears cupped forward. It was so easy to imagine he heard her thoughts.

"Sam? You look utterly transfixed," Ryan said. "Hypnotized. What—?"

Go, Sam thought. *Run, boy*.

How could she have forgotten Ryan had kept Golden Rose, the last of the Kenworthy palominos, for his own, until she and Jen had discovered the hidden stall in the ghost town?

Jen had forgiven him, but Sam felt wary.

Ryan's father would do anything to possess the silver stallion. If Ryan saw him and wanted him, could the Phantom outwit them both?

Sam didn't want Ryan to have even a glimpse of the Phantom.

She forced her eyes skyward. Her mind fumbled for distracting words. She must have looked panicky, not casual, because Ryan turned away in a half crouch, ready for trouble.

"Water!" Sam blurted loudly. "I feel weird. I think I need a drink of water."

But Sam was an awful actress. And a worse liar. Besides, dust hung where the stallion had been. Anyone could see it, and Ryan did.

"What was it?" he demanded. "Tell me."

Hotspot kept Sam from lying.

As if she'd just now caught the stallion's scent, the Appaloosa rushed forward at a trot. Snorting, she stopped beside Sam.

"A mustang," Sam admitted. "I told you they were up here."

Ryan looked thoughtful, not excited. Did you have to be Western born to love mustangs, to feel the vaulting excitement and a yearning to run beside them, if only in your dreams?

Sam didn't think so, but Ryan's handsome face remained blank.

Hotspot's didn't. Head leveled as if she were frozen in a gallop, the mare stared after the mustang. When Sam tried to give Hotspot a gentle pat, the mare shook her head and moved out of reach.

"It wouldn't be the worst thing that could happen," Ryan said.

Was he talking to himself?

"What wouldn't be the worst thing?" Sam asked.

Ryan hesitated, then came out with it.

"If Hotspot were to be taken into some stallion's herd."

Sam had just about gathered the strength to tell Ryan, again, why it was a really bad idea, when her eyes strayed to her watch.

"Oh my gosh, I've got to get back. Dad and Brynna could be there already. Ryan, help me get this stuff picked up. We're starting back. Now!"

He laughed at her order, then hurried to obey.

"It will be quicker getting back to the Jeep than it was climbing up," Ryan promised. "I'll get you home in time, honest."

He sounded determined, but twice as they slipped and slid back down the hillside, Sam caught Ryan looking behind them with a strangely thoughtful expression.

When they reached the truck, Ryan squatted behind it, trying to unhook the horse trailer from the Jeep.

"This isn't as easy as it looks," he muttered.

"What are you doing?" Sam fidgeted, shuffling her feet in the dust as she looked down on him. When he still didn't answer, she suggested, "Just leave it on."

Ryan shook his head. "Returning home with an empty horse trailer would make my father suspicious."

"I don't see why," Sam said. "You were supposed to leave Hotspot at Sterling Stables for a few days, right?"

"And then there's Boots," Ryan said.

"You promised me you were going to talk with your father," Sam reminded him.

"This is time well spent. We'll be faster without the trailer, and you *are* in a hurry," Ryan said.

He might be right, but Sam couldn't shrug off her impatience, especially when he began muttering again.

". . . wires go to brake lights . . ."

Sam's hands curled into tighter fists. Could she possibly reach home before Dad and Brynna? If not, she'd be in trouble, and she'd have an audience for it.

Jen would be there, and so would Mikki and the new HARP girl, Gina.

Oh, she'd make a great impression. She'd be late, in trouble, and—she tried an experimental smile, then gasped in pain—she'd have a black eye from Tempest's hoof.

"Just leave the trailer on," Sam ordered.

Again, Ryan gave a stubborn shake of his head.

"That thing has beaten you. Admit it."

"Give it a rest," Ryan snarled. "I won't be beaten by an inanimate object."

Could she just shove Ryan away from the trailer hitch and drag him to the driver's seat? Sam was considering it when Ryan gave a triumphant laugh.

"Got it!" he said, standing to rub greasy hands together.

He leaned his weight against the horse trailer and shoved the bolt closed, but Sam was already climbing into the Jeep and snapping her seat belt.

As soon as Ryan started the truck, Sam began formulating the script for her talk with Jen. First, she'd ask why Jen had told Ryan about the box canyon in the first place. Next, she'd ask why Jen thought the horses would be safe in the box canyon. Last, she'd recommend that Jen upgrade her taste in guys.

Chapter Five ⬎

Sam stood by the kitchen sink, chugging down a third glass of water. Ryan had dropped her at the River Bend bridge and sped away.

Sam had missed lunch, but Gram hadn't seemed to care. She'd just looked up from pulling weeds in her garden long enough to ask, "How's that cut?"

So Sam made her own lunch, slicing a slab of wheat bread from the loaf, then smearing it with cherry jam and peanut butter. It had been a fine lunch, but it had only magnified her thirst.

"Jen's here," Gram called from outside.

Sam peered out in time to see Silk Stockings, a palomino mare so skittish that Jen called her Silly, jog across the ranch yard.

"Yes!" Sam said to herself. This was going to work out great.

Dad and Brynna had called to say they'd been delayed at the airport. She and Jen would have time to turn Silly out into the ten-acre pasture, choose the beds they wanted in the bunkhouse before the other girls arrived, and still be able to discuss Ryan and the hidden horses.

Sam knew she'd have to be a little bit careful when they talked about Ryan. Though Jen was analytical and levelheaded regarding most subjects, she had a major crush on Ryan. That might force logic to take a backseat to affection.

"Hi!" Sam called. As she hurried outside and stepped down from the porch, the first thing she noticed was Jen's clothes.

She wasn't wearing any eye-searing neon colors.

Instead, Jen wore fresh jeans and a blue flowered shirt. Was she trying to look more adult for her first day as a HARP counselor?

As she dismounted, Jen glanced over her shoulder, and gave Sam an appraising look, too.

"You trying to look tougher than the HARP girls?" Jen asked as she tossed her reins over the hitching rail.

"No," Sam said slowly. *Tougher?* What could Jen mean? Then, she remembered her bandaged cheek. "Oh, this? I just had a disagreement with Tempest."

Jen gave her a half smile. "Does it hurt?"

"Not really."

"Good thing," Jen said, and rushed toward Sam. "This is going to be so fun!"

Jen's white-blond braids flew as she twirled Sam in a hug.

"Absolutely!" Sam answered, and when they stood back to grin at each other, she saw Jen's shirt more clearly.

It wasn't a bit grown-up.

The dark blue on Jen's pale denim shirt wasn't flowers. The pattern was made up of slogans. "Ornery cowgirl," "Shut up and ride," and "Bronc rider in braids." Silhouettes of cowgirls in action were interspersed with the words.

"I love your shirt!" Sam said, turning Jen so that she could read each saying.

"This one's for you." Jen looked down and pointed to a design near her right shoulder.

"'Doin' the moo cow boogie,'" Sam read.

The illustration next to that one showed a cowgirl entangled in her own rope with a crazy cow bucking on the other end.

"You're funny," Sam said, then stuck her tongue out at Jen, who knew she really needed practice at roping.

Still smiling, Jen swept the ten-acre pasture with her gaze, then leaned right and stared past Sam, toward the barn.

"Are they in there?" Jen asked quietly.

Sam didn't ask who *they* were. She knew Jen was talking about Ryan's horses.

"No," Sam said.

"In the round pen?" Jen guessed, with a blush.

Sam hadn't meant her tone to sound as if Jen were simpleminded, but *she'd* been the one to tell Ryan about the box canyon, so she should know where the horses were.

"You girls have everything under control?" Gram asked as she came over, wiping her earth-smeared hands on her jeans.

Jen continued to look around the ranch yard. Then she began to frown.

Sam felt queasy. She'd known something wasn't right! But Gram was waiting for an answer.

"Yep, we've planned everything," Sam said. "Since Mikki's handled Dark Sunshine before, she'll work with Jake every morning, gentling Sunny."

"If Jake cooperates," Jen grumbled.

"He'd better," Sam said, "because we'll be working with Gina. I don't know how much she's ridden, but Popcorn will be nice to her."

"Of course he will," Gram said. "That horse pays back every moment of kindness you give him."

"Jen and I will take turns instructing Gina. Like, Jen will tell her what to do on Popcorn, while I show her on Ace," Sam rushed on.

"In the afternoons the girls will switch," Jen explained. "Mikki will ride Popcorn while Jake instructs and I'll demonstrate on Penny."

"While they do that, Gina and I will gentle Tempest. If she's nice," Sam added.

"Is that cheek feeling pretty sore?" Gram asked.

For a second, Sam didn't understand how Gram's question fit in. Then, she did.

"I didn't mean Tempest," Sam told her. "Of course *she'll* be nice. I was talking about Gina!"

Gram laughed and so did Jen, but Sam could tell her friend was still eager to find out what had happened to the missing Appaloosas.

"I should have guessed that," Gram said. "But you remember to keep that cut clean, dear." Then she gave them each a hug, making sure her soiled gloves didn't dirty their shirts. "Good job, girls."

"Congratulate us later," Jen said. "It's all theory so far. Don't forget we have to get Jake to talk to the girls. And we have to keep our fingers crossed that the girls are teachable."

"They will be," Sam said. "At least Mikki. She's so proud to be coming back as a reward for finishing her classes, and she loves Popcorn."

As Gram waved and returned to her garden, Jen lowered her voice near a whisper. "Where did you put them?"

"Where did you tell him to put them?"

"Here," Jen said gesturing with one hand.

"He said you told him about the box canyon."

"I did, but—" Behind her perfectly clean glasses,

Jen's blue eyes widened. "Don't tell me you left Hotspot and Shy Boots up there?"

"Because you *said* to—"

"I did not!"

"He said, you said—"

"Sam, you of all people know better than that!" Jen's voice soared in amazement. "Even if *I'd* suffered total brain failure, *you've* been attacked by a cougar, you know—"

"Everything all right, girls?" Gram called.

"Well, we've got to go get them," Jen insisted. "That's all there is to it."

"Ryan said he would, as soon as he's had it out with his dad."

Jen sighed. "I don't know, Sam. Linc's in Winnemucca. Didn't he tell you?"

"When he gets back, Ryan's going to confront him."

Jen's expression was a mix of skepticism and hope.

Since they'd ignored her question, Gram returned to listen. "Are you talking about the HARP girls?"

"Yeah," Jen said. "What did she do?"

The conversation was switching around too quickly. Sam pressed the heels of her hands to her temples as she asked, "Who?"

"Gina, the other HARP girl," Jen said, gently.

"I've already heard this sad story," Gram said.

"She's a burglar," Sam said, watching as Gram walked away.

"A b—" Jen's eyes widened once more. "A twelve-year-old girl burglar?"

"Yep."

"That's like real criminal behavior."

"Criminal," Sam pronounced the word slowly. "Like someone who'd steal two horses?"

Jen glanced after Gram.

"It's not the same thing at all, Sam," Jen said, once she was sure Gram was out of earshot. "Those horses belong to the Slocums. He didn't steal them. This is a family problem. I mean, my parents were talking about it before they left, wondering if Ryan would do something."

"Well, he did," Sam said.

"I know, and I'm proud of him," Jen said. "In a twisted, pathetic way, it's the right thing to do."

Sam smiled. This sounded more like Jen.

"He should have talked Linc out of this or gotten help from another adult—like your dad," Sam said.

When Jen's hands perched on her hips, Sam knew she'd gone too far in criticizing the boy Jen liked.

"Look, Sam," Jen said, "can you always make your dad see your point of view?"

"Of course not—"

"Neither can I, and Ryan can't, either. In fact, I think he has more trouble in that department than we do."

Sam nodded energetically, but kept her lips pressed together.

"Still, what he did is no big deal. Neither of you did anything wrong. No one can say you did."

Just then, Blaze crawled out from the cool shade under the bunkhouse porch. He frisked through the flock of Rhode Island Red hens, then turned toward the bridge.

His tail-wagging, open-mouthed greeting had to mean Dad and Brynna were coming.

Sam wished she were that excited to face her parents, but she wasn't.

Gram's yellow Buick bumped over the River Bend bridge, driven by Dad. Sam could see a flurry of backseat movement from here and despite her worry, she smiled. She didn't know about Gina, but she could guess Mikki would be going nuts.

After a rocky start, Mikki had grown to love everything about River Bend Ranch, especially the horses.

Dad had barely stopped the car when a door burst open and Mikki emerged. She seemed to roll out and onto her feet like a stunt woman.

"Sam!" Mikki shouted, but she didn't run over to her.

Mikki whirled, arms outstretched, as if she'd hug the white house, the horses, the cottonwood trees, and the watering troughs. "Oh my gosh, this is like a dream!"

As Mikki threw back her head for a deep breath, her wispy blond hair looked like disheveled feathers.

Her arms curled around her ribs, hugging herself as if even the smell of the ranch delighted her.

"Is she crazy?" Jen asked quietly.

"Maybe," Sam said, "but I'm the same kind of crazy. I felt just like that when I got back from San Francisco."

Mikki burst into a run that took her halfway across the ranch yard. Then suddenly she skidded to a stop. She looked back at the girl who was just climbing out of the car.

Impatiently, Mikki rubbed her palms on her jeans and waited.

Maybe she was just being considerate of the other girl, but Sam guessed Mikki had felt suddenly self-conscious.

Maybe seeing Jen or remembering Gina reminded Mikki that she and Sam didn't know each other that well.

Despite the voice in her conscience urging her to confess the horse theft to Dad, Sam wanted Mikki to enjoy their reunion, so she resisted the urge to run over to the car while Dad was getting out.

"C'mon," Sam said, touching Jen's arm. "You'll like Mikki—if you remember she's three years younger than we are, and she hasn't done that well in school."

"I'm not a show-off, am I?" Jen asked.

"Of course not," Sam said.

Jen couldn't help how smart she was, but Sam

knew from Mikki's last trip here in October that she got defensive when she didn't understand something.

Jen kept walking.

"Thanks, I won't make her feel dumb." Jen pushed her glasses up her nose. "That's what you meant, right?"

"Well, yeah," Sam admitted. "But in the nicest possible way."

"I can do that," Jen said.

Mikki was tinier than Sam remembered. Her head reached about an inch above Sam's shoulder.

Clearly uneasy, Mikki raised her chin and put her hands on her hips, but she didn't wear the "grudge against the world" glare she'd had before.

In fact, Sam thought, if she'd been in Mikki's place, she'd feel kind of cranky, too, guessing Jen probably knew the worst about her—like the fact that she'd gotten into the HARP program by being a bad kid, and she'd nearly burned down the River Bend barn with a carelessly tossed cigarette.

Now, Mikki yawned as if she didn't really care, but her eyes were wary.

"I'm so glad to see you." Sam gave Mikki's shoulders a one-armed hug, then she turned back to Jen. "Mikki, this is Jen Kenworthy. She's a world-class rider, a future vet, and my best friend. That gorgeous palomino mare over there is hers, and both of them are going to be here all week."

Silly turned her golden head as far from the

hitching rack as her reins would allow, then nickered.

"She's beautiful," Mikki sighed, and Jen and Sam laughed in a shared feeling.

Someone who didn't love horses might scold Mikki for talking about Silly before acknowledging the introduction to Jen. Among the three of them, though, that made perfect sense.

"And she knows it," Jen said as the mare shook her creamy mane and pawed with a front hoof. "Her name is Silk Stockings, but we call her Silly." When Mikki made a despairing sound, Jen added, "Silly has a well-earned reputation for being ditzy."

Mikki looked down, as if the mention of reputation had stirred her embarrassment.

"I don't know what anybody's told you about me, but I'm not like that anymore," Mikki said. "This semester at school I made up all the credits I lost from cutting and stuff, and I passed all my new classes, too."

"Sounds like you worked harder than I did," Sam said.

"I did it so I come back here," Mikki said, still watching Jen. "So, I don't want you thinking I'm a screwup."

"No, *I'm* the screwup."

Sam turned toward the voice and saw a girl who looked like a boy.

Sam took the thought back almost instantly.

A blue baseball cap hid her hair, dark glasses

covered her eyes, and a loose T-shirt nearly reached the knees of her jeans. She was thin and agile looking, too, but Gina's face was rosy and pretty.

"Hi, I'm Sam and this is my friend Jen. We—"

"*I'm* Gina Lucca."

The girl crossed her arms and tapped her foot.

Sam stood speechless. So did Jen. Gina was obviously waiting for the recognition due to a celebrity.

"Gina Lucca?" She repeated, then slipped off her sunglasses to reveal long black eyelashes that actually cast shadows on her cheeks.

She was cute, Sam thought, but she wasn't famous. Was she?

The girl gave a dramatic sigh.

"Perhaps you know me better as the Baseball Burglar."

Chapter Six ❧

Sam opened her mouth, but nothing came out. Should she admit she'd never heard of the Baseball Burglar?

Mikki groaned and rolled her eyes, but Jen had a different reaction. She took the announcement as an invitation to pry.

"Baseball Burglar? What's that mean?"

"It means, that's what they called me in the newspaper, and on the local TV news," Gina bragged.

Sam glanced back toward the Buick where Dad and Brynna stood talking, clearly letting the girls get to know each other before they interrupted, but she would have loved a little advice.

"They know all about me," Gina said, as she

caught the direction of Sam's glance.

"Oh, no, I was just—" Sam began.

"Anyone with ears and the bad luck to get within twenty feet of her knows all about her," Mikki said.

"So you don't mind talking about"—Jen paused— "what got you into the HARP program?"

"Mind? She can't shut up about it," Mikki said.

"Can I help it if I've had a fascinating life?" Gina gloated.

Sam laughed at the self-centered twelve-year-old, but Jen rubbed her palms together as if she couldn't wait to get all the juicy details of Gina's crimes.

"So, why are you called the Baseball Burglar, instead of the Cat Burglar or, considering your age, even the Baby Burglar?"

Sam thought Gina would be embarrassed or irritated by that last suggestion, but she wasn't.

"It's because of my . . ." Gina paused as if awaiting a fanfare, "modus operandi."

"Like, the way you do it?" Sam asked. She'd heard the phrase on television mysteries, but she wasn't sure what it meant.

"The way I enter the scene, what I do once I'm inside the house," Gina said airily. "That sort of thing."

Sam's amusement faded as she realized Gina wasn't embarrassed. Shouldn't she be ashamed of doing something so stupid and wrong?

Sam thought of the cozy kitchen at River Bend. She pictured the couch where she sprawled to watch television with her cat Cougar purring beside her.

Sam imagined a stranger sneaking up the staircase to her room. Would she ever feel the same about home if someone broke in?

She glared at Gina. People had a right to feel relaxed and secure in their houses. Did Gina get a kick out of wrecking that for them?

"Let's go see the horses," Mikki said.

"Good idea," Sam answered, but first she met Jen's eyes, expecting a reflection of her own anger.

Jen didn't take her eyes off Gina. She seemed to consider the girl as if she were a math problem.

"So, tell me about the baseball part of it," Jen said. Her voice was totally inviting, not condemning at all.

Gina turned cautious. "You sound like the psychologist they sent me to."

"Right," Jen stretched the word out with sarcasm. "That would be me. A kid who lives on a ranch in the middle of nowhere, but is actually a psychologist!"

"Well, you are a counselor here," Gina defended her suspicion.

"Because I can ride a horse," Jen said.

"Okay." Gina shrugged. "What I do is this: after school, I scope out really nice houses that look like they're empty."

"Abandoned?" Sam asked.

Gina shook her head.

"No, the people are off at work. Then, just to be sure—wait, I forgot to tell you I always look like this." Gina swept a hand past her cap, T-shirt, and jeans. "If I didn't"—Gina yanked off her cap and swoopy brown waves of hair fell to her shoulders—"people would notice me walking along with a bat and ball. So"—she tugged the cap back into place—"I always wear it."

"Ingenious," Jen said.

"Whatever," Gina said, looking irritated. "Then I throw up the ball," she said, pantomiming the action, "Swing, and slug it through a window."

"A back window?" Sam asked.

"Back, front, whatever," Gina said. "And if no one comes running out to see what no-good kid did it, I break in. And because I look so young," she smirked at Jen, "I don't get in trouble if anyone sees me."

"Why not?" Jen asked.

"I just cry and pretend I was trying to get my ball back."

"Using people's stereotypes against them," Jen muttered, then she looked up at Mikki. "We'll go see the horses in just a second, but Gina, I've got to know. What do you steal?"

"Candy," Gina said with a nod of satisfaction.

"Candy?" Sam yelped. "You risk going to jail just for candy?"

"I've heard enough," Mikki said. "I'm going to see the horses."

"Me too," Sam said, and she felt a surge of satis-faction when Gina tried to regather her audience.

"Not just jelly beans and—" Gina called after them.

"There he is!" Mikki yelled.

"Hey, don't you want to know—"

But Mikki was already jogging ahead toward the ten-acre pasture, so Sam hurried to catch her.

When she caught up, Sam found Mikki's eyes taking in all the horses.

Popcorn stood closest, almost as he had this morn-ing, and Sam had the totally impossible feeling that the albino mustang had been waiting all day for Mikki.

At the sound of approaching feet, Sam looked over to see Brynna coming toward the pasture as Dad departed for the barn with just a wave.

If Mikki had had enough of Gina's burglar brag-ging, Dad was probably nuts from it.

"Everything go all right while we were gone?" Brynna asked.

Sam took a deep breath, ready to start her con-fession.

But a closer look at Brynna made her reconsider.

Although Sam's stepmother wore a cheery pink dress and her red hair was fastened neatly back with a clip, she looked tired. Brynna was in charge of the Willow Springs Wild Horse Center, where hundreds of fresh-off-the-range mustangs were kept until they were adopted. She worked with the ranch horses and the HARP program, too.

Brynna looked like she needed a nap, not an explanation of how Sam had hidden two horses in a scheme that would bring a neighbor's anger crashing down on them.

Sam decided to wait and tell Dad as soon as she could.

"Everything went fine," Sam told Brynna. "Except that Dallas and I disagreed about the right way to teach Tempest to lead."

"Does he have a black eye, too?" Brynna asked, smiling.

Sam's hand darted up to touch her cheek.

"No, but I won." Sam laughed. "Actually, I just, uh, bumped into Tempest's hoof."

Brynna winced, then glanced toward the barn. "You'd better come up with something better than that before you talk with your dad."

Sam nodded and Brynna's attention shifted back to Popcorn and Mikki.

"He looks good, doesn't he?" Brynna said.

Still staring at the albino, Mikki sighed and said, "Wonderful."

"Good food, kind treatment, and a fair amount of work," Brynna explained. "You'll be riding him soon."

"I'm not in a hurry," Mikki said. "I wasn't that good at it."

"You'll be better by the end of the week," Sam said, and when Brynna touched her shoulder in approval, Sam tried to believe she deserved it.

She didn't get to bask in her stepmother's silent praise for long.

Suddenly Brynna looked past her, toward the entrance to River Bend Ranch.

"What on earth is that?"

Sam looked over her shoulder in time to see a huge yellow Hummer rumble their way. Immediately, she recognized the vehicle Ryan had waved to when they'd been taking the horses to the box canyon.

"I think I know *who* it is," Sam told Brynna. "The guy who owns the deerhounds."

Brynna's blue eyes narrowed and she cast a quick look toward the barn, just as Dad and Dallas emerged.

"Can you remember his name?" Brynna asked, and Sam noticed every bit of her stepmother's weariness fall away. Brisk and official, she might have put on her uniform.

For a minute, Sam's mind came up with nothing but an insect. Sort of like a grasshopper made of dry sticks. A praying mantis, that was it. As the image crossed her mind, Sam wondered if the word was spelled *pray* or *prey*.

"Karl Mannix," Jen said, coming up to stand beside them. "Sam, remember I told you about him?"

"Yeah, so did Ryan," Sam said.

"He still works for Linc? After that deer hound fiasco?" Brynna asked as the Hummer parked next to Gram's Buick.

"Yes," Jen said.

"Deer hounds?" Gina said, but she must have sensed the tension among the others, because she didn't press for more information, just sidled closer to Mikki, who shrugged as Karl Mannix came toward them.

Despite the hot July day, Sam shivered.

Lanky and tall, Karl Mannix was dressed in outdoor clothes that fit, but didn't suit him. Ryan had quoted Jen's dad as saying the man knew more about stocks and bonds than livestock, and Sam's first glimpse of him made her agree.

He might be dressed like a cowboy, but he didn't move like one. In fact, as Karl Mannix crossed the ranch yard, he gave her the creeps.

Dehydration or imagination made her think she heard his bones sliding against each other as he approached.

Or maybe it was guilt, Sam thought. After all, if he'd paid attention, this guy — Linc Slocum's employee — had seen her in the very act of taking the Appaloosas.

He doesn't look threatening, Sam scolded herself. With his beaked nose and water-blue eyes behind his thick glasses, he looked like a nerd.

"You have police out here?" Gina asked.

"Indeed we do," Brynna said. "Here comes Sheriff Ballard."

Brynna's tone was conversational as the sheriff's black-and-white patrol car bumped over the River

Bend bridge, but Sam wasn't fooled.

Brynna bristled with a warning that said Sam had better not have anything to do with these unexpected visitors.

And things were about to get worse.

Sam's ribs tightened like a vise around her lungs as Linc Slocum's beige Cadillac sped over the bridge, fishtailing as he sawed at the steering wheel, trying to follow the sheriff.

If Ryan had talked with his father, things hadn't gone well.

With his rolling cowboy's gait, Dad came to stand between Sam and Brynna.

Sam remembered crossing her arms and stubbornly refusing to help Ryan. That had been just this morning. She wished she could turn back time, so she'd be standing here enjoying the excitement instead of regretting she'd ever met Ryan Slocum.

"Shoot, if I'd known the circus was comin' to town, I woulda got us home earlier," Dad said.

Sam and Jen gave forced laughs, but Mikki and Gina looked frightened and Gram's face was strained as she welcomed the HARP girls and tried to ignore the three cars crowding the ranch yard.

This might not have anything to do with the horses, Sam told herself. *Ryan promised he'd take the blame.*

"I didn't do anything," Mikki said.

"Me either," Gina said.

"Good thing, or you two woulda been on a bus

bound for home first thing tomorrow morning," Dad joked.

"He's kidding," Brynna said at the girls' startled expressions.

While Brynna reassured them, Jen sidled closer to Sam.

"I'm sorry I ever told him a thing," Jen apologized. "But this could be about something else, don't you think?"

Sam shook her head "no." She didn't.

When Linc's Cadillac barreled around the other car, convincing Karl Mannix to jump out of his path, and Blaze to sprint under the bunkhouse porch, Sam knew she was in big trouble.

Linc pulled up just yards away, instead of parking across the ranch yard alongside the other vehicles.

The Cadillac's door swung open, hit the limit of its hinges, and rebounded, slamming closed before Linc could get out.

"This is gonna be fun," Jen muttered.

The Cadillac's door didn't stay closed for long.

Linc Slocum's hair was slicked back and glossy as patent leather. As he stood next to his car, his face shone red under skin so tight, it looked as if he might explode out of it.

"Where are my horses?" he bellowed. "I want to know right now!"

Chapter Seven ൶

Sam noticed Sheriff Ballard's leisurely approach.

The Rhode Island Red hens had scattered at the boom of Linc's voice, so there was no doubt Sheriff Ballard had heard it, too, but his stride didn't falter as he walked toward them.

Linc Slocum might be closer, standing right in front of Sam, her family, Jen, and the HARP girls, but it was clear Sheriff Ballard would be in charge when he reached them.

Before anyone else could speak, Gram greeted Linc in her most neighborly voice.

"Hello, Linc. I just baked some oatmeal cookies. I hope you have time for a few."

"Grace, I don't want to hurt your feelings, but I

didn't come for cookies. This kid of yours is a horse thief!"

Sam gasped as if he'd knocked the breath out of her. When Brynna's arm rested around her waist, Sam leaned into it. Dad looked like he was counting to ten so that he wouldn't take a swing at Linc.

But Linc was almost right.

"Oh, now Linc . . ." Gram began patiently.

"'Now Linc' nothin'," he began, but Dad's stern voice cut him off.

"'Afternoon, Linc. You mighta noticed we have company." Dad nodded at Mikki and Gina. "For their sake, I'll thank you to get a grip on your temper."

Linc respected Dad, and it showed in his sudden embarrassment.

"Pardon me," Linc said.

But Dad wasn't done with him. "I'll be real curious to hear you explain yourself to Sheriff Ballard, too," Dad said. Behind him, Dallas crossed his arms, seconding Dad's statement.

Sam felt sick. She wanted to disappear. Dad, Gram, and Brynna were standing up for her, and though Linc wasn't exactly right, he wasn't completely wrong.

Mikki chewed the cuticle on her thumbnail while Gina picked at a thread on the seam of her jeans. Their tension said this wasn't what they'd expected at a sleepy Nevada ranch.

Sam felt blame gathering on her shoulders.

"Hello, folks." Sheriff Ballard's easy greeting didn't match the cold eyes that seemed to touch them all—Dad and Brynna first, then Dallas and Gram, the HARP girls, Jen, and, it really seemed like he looked at her last, Sam thought—before he faced Linc Slocum.

"Go ahead," the sheriff said then, and Sam hoped it was good news that Sheriff Ballard's voice was filled with forced patience.

Maybe, because Linc Slocum had been in so much trouble before, the sheriff wouldn't listen to what he said.

But behind the sheriff, outside the half circle of people facing the sheriff and Linc, was Karl Mannix.

Sam's pulse stampeded when he looked directly at her and nodded without smiling.

He couldn't have seen her clearly as he went driving by on the highway, could he? Oh, why had Ryan waved at him?

Even though Mannix stood behind Sheriff Ballard, Sam felt certain the sheriff knew Mannix was there.

"Ryan was supposed to load up my Appy mare in the horse van and take her back over to Sterling Stables today," Linc explained. "I told him to leave that half-breed colt behind to wean himself."

Sam listened to each syllable Linc uttered. So far, his story matched Ryan's, but he hadn't yet admitted he wanted to destroy the colt.

"When I got home from Winnemucca, the mare and colt were gone, and the Cherokee is still there. What do you make of that?" Linc demanded.

"Ryan was here with the colt," Gram said, "and it was plain to see he's fond of that young horse, so they're probably together."

On either side of Sam, Brynna and Dad pulled away slightly. She could almost hear them wondering what Ryan and Shy Boots had been doing here, but they didn't ask.

"Have you spoken to Ryan?" Gram asked Linc.

Sam held her breath.

"Not before he left," Linc said, then shrugged. "But that's not the point."

Linc kept talking, but his words no longer sunk into Sam's whirling mind.

Jen had grabbed her hand and was squeezing it, hard.

Sam wet her lips and found she was able to pronounce one word. "Left?"

"Don't pretend you don't know," Linc said. "Or you either," he added, turning on Jen.

"You mean Ryan's gone now?" Sam asked. "Where?"

"You know darned well where. Shopping and whatnot with his twin and their mother, who just flew in from London."

Sam shook her head. This couldn't be happening. She glanced at Jen. If she'd known . . . But her best friend's hand covered her lips and her eyes were wide and blinking behind the lenses of her glasses.

"Maybe you could just ask him—" Sam began.

"He left an hour ago . . ."

Ryan had been afraid his father would do something to Shy Boots if he wasn't around to protect the colt, but he hadn't said he was leaving today.

". . . mother's private plane landed at the ranch and took them off to San Francisco. That's how you two had it planned, right?"

Sam knew she was gulping like a beached fish, but she couldn't form words. Why would Ryan leave her to take the blame for stealing the horses?

"Okay Linc, if you're done blowin' off steam, let's start over."

Sam jumped. She'd been so focused on Linc, she'd forgotten Sheriff Ballard. He took out a small notebook and pen, in a routine manner.

"You have two missing horses. That's all I know for sure. Now, forget the speculation. Don't tell me what you think happened, just list the facts, starting when you realized the horses were missing."

"Okay, Sheriff," Linc said. When he squared his shoulders and tugged briskly at his shirt cuffs, Sam felt chills.

She'd rather see Linc ranting.

He must have realized bluster would get him nowhere with Sheriff Ballard, because Linc seemed almost businesslike.

This was a far more threatening Linc Slocum, because the sheriff might take him seriously.

"I realized Apache Hotspot and her foal were missing exactly"—Linc glanced at his heavy gold watch—"thirty-five minutes ago."

"So you called my office right away," Sheriff Ballard said, consulting his notes. "That's good. In cases like this, the first twenty-four hours are critical."

"Do you have any fences down?" Dallas asked. "Were the front gates to your place open?"

"They didn't wander away, if that's what you're thinkin'," Linc said.

"When did you see them last?" Sheriff Ballard continued.

"Last night," Linc said. "We—that's Ryan and I— were standing in the barn discussing how he was supposed to take the mare to Sterling Stables and leave her to be bred."

"And now Ryan's out of town," the sheriff said.

"Yes sir," Linc answered.

Sheriff Ballard looked up from his notes. "So, he could've taken the horses to Sterling Stables before-hand."

Linc looked uneasy. Though he wasn't much of a father, he didn't want any blame placed on Ryan.

All he said was, "The mare never got there."

Sheriff Ballard exhaled loudly.

"Okay, the first thing we need to do—" Sheriff Ballard began.

"Sheriff, excuse me. This is where I need to step in." Karl Mannix did just that, taking a stride forward.

Sheriff Ballard nodded as if he'd been expecting this interruption.

Karl Mannix cleared his throat, then introduced himself. While Sheriff Ballard made notes, Mannix explained he was employed by Linc Slocum, then turned to the day's events.

"It's true Ryan didn't want that mare taken from her foal," Mannix said. He paused, blinking. His eyes looked watery behind his glasses. "But earlier today, I saw him with this young lady."

Mannix cleared his throat again. Was he trying to underline the significance of seeing her with Ryan?

"You know how Samantha is," Linc said, keeping his voice level. "She convinced him to turn the Appys loose to run with that wild bunch."

"No, I did not!"

Sheriff Ballard held up his hand. "Linc, that's the kind of speculation I want you to avoid."

"Of course," Linc said. "Sorry."

But he looked satisfied that he'd made his point.

"You're sure it was Samantha you saw with Ryan?" Sheriff Ballard asked Mannix.

"Pretty sure," Mannix said.

"It was me," Sam said.

"Well, what if she did go out for a drive with him?" Gram tsked her tongue. "I said it was fine."

Beside her, Dad sighed. He sounded disappointed, and that hurt.

"It just seemed strange to me that Ryan would be way out here, when he was supposed to be dropping the mare off so far in the opposite direction," Mannix said. "So when Mr. Slocum got home from Winnemucca, I asked him about it. We checked to see if all his stock was accounted for, and you know the rest."

The air might have been full of bees, for the buzzing Sam heard in her ears.

Why hadn't she told Ryan no? She should have stood up to him, and it was pretty ironic that she hadn't, since she'd always thought *he* showed no backbone.

"With Ryan being a newcomer, and Samantha's reputation for loving wild horses . . ." Linc let his voice trail off, hoping the sheriff would reach the wrong conclusion.

Mannix gave an indulgent smile. Sam felt everyone's eyes on her as he added, "Well, what boy hasn't let a pretty girl talk him into—"

"Do I get to say anything?" Sam demanded.

"I think you'd better," Sheriff Ballard told her.

"Wait just a minute," Brynna interrupted. "Before Sam says a word, I'm going to." Brynna gave Sheriff Ballard a stern look that said she was depending on him to see her as a fellow professional. He gave a slight nod. "Sam knows what can happen when a wild stallion takes on a mare with a foal that isn't his.

She wouldn't turn Hotspot and her foal loose on the range."

Sam swallowed hard. If they couldn't believe in her honesty, they'd still believe in her soft heart for horses.

If there hadn't been so many people standing around, she would have given Brynna a hug.

"I wouldn't do that," Sam agreed. "Honest."

Sheriff Ballard met her eyes. "Tell me what did happen."

"The horses weren't stolen," Sam insisted. "And they're not lost."

When her eyes strayed to Jen's, Sam saw the tug-of-war between her friend's loyalties.

"Sam," the sheriff said seriously, "I didn't ask what didn't happen."

"Right," she said.

"She's protecting someone," Jen blurted.

Mikki and Gina gave uneasy laughs. In a way, Sam didn't blame them. Jen's words sounded kind of dramatic, like something you'd hear on television.

"Go ahead and tell," Jen told her.

Sam stared toward the barn corral, hoping for a glimpse of Tempest between the fence rails. The flicker of shiny black comforted her and made her feel a little stronger.

"Ryan brought Shy Boots—that's Hotspot's foal," she explained to the sheriff, "over to play with Tempest."

"Of all the—" Linc began, then clamped his lips shut.

"While Ryan was here . . ." Sam said, then swallowed. This was hard to do with just the facts. "He asked me to help hide Hotspot and Shy Boots."

"Did he say why?" the sheriff asked.

"He was afraid his father was going to get rid of Shy Boots while Hotspot was at Sterling Stables."

"Is that what you think, or what he said?"

"He said his father was embarrassed when Hotspot bit and kicked Cloud Cap, and when the Sterlings said it might be easier after the foal was weaned. And Ryan overheard his father talking on the phone to someone this morning, saying the easiest way to wean Shy Boots was to *cull* him."

"Is that so?" the sheriff asked.

"I'm afraid not," Linc said. "I left home for Winnemucca long before Ryan was awake, and I didn't talk with anyone before I hit the road. I did plan to wean the colt early, but I only meant to pasture it where the mare couldn't see it."

Sheriff Ballard held up a hand to halt Linc's long-winded defense.

"And so, Samantha, you took the horses somewhere," Sheriff Ballard said.

"Up to a box canyon on the way to Cowkiller Caldera," Sam admitted. "And I was just about to tell my dad, because I didn't think they'd be safe up there overnight."

Dad rubbed the back of his neck and scuffed one boot in the dirt. "I wonder why ya took 'em up there, then."

"Ryan wouldn't take no for an answer," Sam said, but when Dad exhaled and shook his head, she heard how lame her excuse sounded.

The sheriff closed his notebook with a snap.

"Doesn't sound like a crime's been committed. It's inconvenient, but a family matter.

"Linc, since he caused the inconvenience, you might think of sending your boy up there to retrieve those horses, soon as he gets home."

"That'll be a few days," Linc said. "And I still say he's not to blame."

"They can't stay up there overnight," Sam protested.

"You're thinking of coyotes and cougars," Dad said. "She's got a point. Even if you leave now, Linc, it'll be dark by the time you get there."

They all glanced up. Dusk was falling. Against the purple-gray sky, a bat flickered out from the barn's loft.

"They'll be fine," Linc said.

They won't be fine, Sam thought. But Ryan had been right. Linc had already lost interest in Hotspot.

Karl Mannix hadn't. He cleared his throat, attracting everyone's attention.

"Sheriff, if you'll lead the way, I'll follow you up there and bring the horses back."

"The trailer's still up there," Sam said.

"That's handy," Karl Mannix said.

Sheriff Ballard stuck his pen in his shirt pocket. "Shouldn't take but a few minutes. If it's okay with you," he said to Dad and Brynna, "I'll have Sam ride along to point out the canyon. With it coming on dark, I don't want to miss it."

When Dad nodded, the sheriff said, "Let's go, Samantha."

"But Mikki and Gina," Sam said. "I have to help get them settled and—"

"We can handle things without you," Brynna said, sounding almost cold. "This takes precedence."

Sam wasn't sure, but the firm set of Brynna's lips implied that since Sam was supposed to be a role model for the HARP girls, she'd better hurry up and clear her good name.

Chapter Eight ❧

Sam had always thought it would be fun to ride in a police car. It wasn't.

A metal grate loomed behind the seat. She didn't turn to look at it, but it hovered there like a silent threat.

She told herself she was lucky Karl wasn't riding with them. Otherwise Sheriff Ballard might have made her ride in that backseat cage.

"You can let go," Sheriff Ballard said as he drove down the highway along the La Charla River.

Sam didn't know what he meant. Without taking his eyes from the windshield, he reached over and tapped her clasped hands. Sam looked down.

Her fingers were interlaced so tightly, she had to

work them apart. While she did, she thought of how badly she'd messed up this time.

Sheriff Ballard was her friend. He'd helped her solve the mystery of her mother's death and he'd adopted Jinx, the fierce but frightened mustang who'd been a bucking horse. Her misbehavior must be embarrassing for him, just as it was for her family.

"I'm sorry," she said softly.

"I know you did this out of the goodness of your heart," Sheriff Ballard told her. "But you want to put a little more thought into situations like this. Peer pressure—"

"I didn't do it for Ryan; I did it for Shy Boots. I think Ryan's probably right. Linc would have gotten rid of the colt."

"Maybe. And maybe I heard through the grapevine that something like this was brewing."

Sam started to ask who'd told him, but she knew he wouldn't tell.

"Samantha, how'd you get hurt?" he asked suddenly.

Sam's hand darted to her cheek.

"My filly did it," she said, wondering why he cared. "I'm training her to lead."

"You're sure?" he said, and the accusation in his words suddenly made sense.

"Oh my gosh, Ryan didn't bully me into helping him," she said. "Ryan's not that way."

"Never be too sure, Samantha. It's hard to tell

what people will do when they're desperate."

For a minute, Sam heard nothing but the tires on the road.

"It was my filly," she said, finally. "Dallas saw it happen and Gram bandaged it for me. Ryan was actually a little worried about it."

In the car's dimness, the sheriff nodded.

"Ryan might be a fine kid. Maybe he just needs to cowboy up a little bit," the sheriff said a few miles later.

Cowboy up, Sam thought. The expression made her smile even before Sheriff Ballard added, "You know, quit whinin' and do what needs to be done. I'd like to think that's the only problem," the sheriff continued, "but he told you he'd spring these horses by nightfall, Sam, and now he's gone. He's four hundred miles away, for the best part of the week."

"I don't know why he did that," Sam said. Even to her, her voice sounded small inside the rushing police car.

"Because he knows you're the kind of girl who'd do the wrong thing, if it's for the right reason." He paused, letting his words sink in before adding, "He left you holding the bag, Samantha."

"I know."

Sam stared out the window, into the darkness. In that moment, she gave up on Ryan Slocum, for good.

Only the horses mattered now.

❋ ❋ ❋

In the gloomy dusk, Sam almost missed the spot where Ryan had fought so hard to unhitch the trailer.

"There it is," Sam said, pointing, but as the sheriff pulled over and parked, she noticed the trailer was open.

Panic vaulted up in Sam's chest.

"I know it probably doesn't matter," she said, quickly, "but the trailer was latched. The handle on the door . . ." she gestured, showing how Ryan had shoved it into place.

That didn't make sense. She and Ryan were the only ones who'd known the trailer was here. After he'd dropped her off at River Bend Ranch, could he have come back and put the horses inside? Had there been time for him to do that before the private plane arrived for him and Rachel?

Sam jumped out of the police car.

"Don't touch it, Sam," the sheriff said before she could close her door. "Let me."

Fidgeting, Sam watched the sheriff tug a handkerchief from his pocket, but the trailer was silent. She knew the horses weren't inside.

Using the handkerchief to cover his hand, the sheriff opened the trailer door farther. Of course it was empty.

Karl Mannix drove up in the bright-yellow Hummer, lowered his window, and chuckled at the pains the sheriff was taking not to smear fingerprints.

"Just gonna check out this trailer, then Sam and I'll walk up and see that the horses are safe. We'll bring 'em back down."

"How far up is it?" Mannix nodded to the trail.

The sheriff turned, passing the question to Sam.

"About a mile," she said. "It's a rough walk, but not very long."

"Shoot, we can get up there in the Hummer. No need to walk," Karl boasted.

"Let's not rip up the trail," the sheriff said.

"It's nothing but weeds and dirt," Karl insisted.

Sam stared at the vehicle Karl wanted to take up the hill. The Hummer was as big as an apartment on wheels. It could crush squirrel burrows, demolish deerpaths, and terrify mustangs. Even if the wildlife escaped, the plants they lived on would be ripped and mashed.

"Don't want to take a chance on scaring the horses off, if they've broken out," the sheriff added. "They'll probably head downhill, toward home."

"You're the expert," Karl said, and parked. The yellow Hummer glowed in the twilight.

Sheriff Ballard grabbed a heavy flashlight from his car. Before they left, he turned it on, squatted, and played the beam inside the trailer, then over the dirt surrounding it. Sam and Mannix watched until he rose to his feet.

"Sam, is there another way—besides this trail—to

where you left the horses?"

Sam pictured the Phantom's territory, then slowly shook her head.

"Not unless you start out from Arroyo Azul," she said, pointing.

"We'd never make it before dark," Sheriff Ballard said. "I'm just thinking, if this turns out to be a crime scene, I don't want to destroy any more evidence than we have to.

"Mr. Mannix, why don't you just relax in your vehicle? Sam and I can handle whatever we've got here."

For two or three heartbeats, Sam felt better.

"No, I'll come along," Mannix insisted. "Don't think my boss would like it if I stayed behind."

"Why's that?" the sheriff asked.

Sam heard the challenge in Sheriff Ballard's voice. Was Mannix hinting that Linc Slocum didn't trust the sheriff?

But Mannix only said, "Can't have him thinking I'm lazy."

"Okay," Sheriff Ballard said. "But stay off to the left side on the way up. Don't walk on the trail."

Sam led the way. Striding up the rocky shoulder, Sam glanced back in time to see Sheriff Ballard's right hand hover over the gun in its snapped holster.

She sucked in a breath.

This whole situation was unreal. How had helping Ryan and the horses gotten her into this mess?

Sheriff Ballard stayed so close behind, he reached out and steadied her arm when her foot slipped on a rock.

The sheriff was alert, scanning the terrain around them. More than once, he reminded Karl Mannix to stay off the center of the trail.

The first time, Mannix apologized. The second time, he laughed. He wasn't taking this very seriously. He was doing a good job of hiking, though, Sam thought.

She had to walk faster and take longer strides to stay ahead of him. Another glance back showed Sam why she'd thought his outdoor clothes looked a little odd.

Karl Mannix wore cowboy clothes down to his boots. They were hiking boots, which laced around hooks up to his ankles.

As darkness closed in, Sam heard something on the trail ahead and stopped to listen. There was a gentle plop of weight hitting dirt.

"What's going on?" Mannix asked loudly.

Sam held her hand up, listening. It was probably nothing to worry about, but the darkness made her turn to Sheriff Ballard.

"Deer?" he asked under his breath.

"Yeah, of course," she whispered.

Then the creature plunged off the trail and into a thicket of brush.

"Must be," she said. "Jen and I didn't leave any

cattle up here, and I don't think we'd hear a mustang."

"Not if he heard us first," the sheriff said.

Still, with every step she took, Sam's eyes swept the shadows, watching for the Phantom.

He'd been up here just hours ago. Only humans could keep him from stealing Hotspot if he wanted to add her to his harem.

"We're getting close," Sam said at last.

A faint evening breeze rustled the cottonwood leaves ahead, but they heard no questioning nicker from Hotspot or Shy Boots.

She hoped the mare was just dozing, with the foal tucked beside her.

When they were almost there, Sam's steps slowed and Sheriff Ballard clicked on his flashlight.

"Fence is down," he said as the beam struck orange plastic strewn on the ground.

The light lifted, played across the canyon's rock walls, then dropped, hunting over the grass, searching for the horses.

But Sam's hopes had already sunk. The horses were gone.

For a few minutes, Sheriff Ballard examined the plastic fence and the thick branches she and Jen, then she and Ryan, had used as posts.

"Someone took this fence down," the sheriff said flatly.

"How do you know?" Mannix asked. "I bet they

broke out and ran for the hills."

Sam crossed fingers on both hands, hoping Mannix was wrong.

"Horses would jump over, or break through with their chests, pulling the fence through the staples. They sure wouldn't aim for the posts. Whoever got 'em out yanked right here by the posts and popped the staples loose."

Relief coursed through Sam. The Phantom wasn't to blame.

"Amazing," Mannix said with a chuckle, and it struck Sam that he hadn't expected such detailed analysis from a small-town sheriff like Heck Ballard.

"Should we have Jake come up and look for tracks?" Sam asked.

"No," Sheriff Ballard said. "Ryan wanted to keep the horses from his dad. This is for them to work out."

"Yeah," Mannix seconded.

"I don't know how he would've had time," Sam protested.

"He might've hired some help," Sheriff Ballard said. "After all, look how he turned to you."

It sounded nice, put that way, but Sam knew Sheriff Ballard was repeating what he'd told her before. If Ryan had left her holding the bag, why wouldn't he hire someone else to take the horses?

The walk back down was quiet as the three concentrated on putting their feet in safe places on the steep trail.

"Sheriff, I'll just hitch up that trailer and be on my way," Mannix said when they reached level ground again.

"Leave it here," Sheriff Ballard said, and when Mannix looked startled, he added, "I want another look at it in the daylight. You never know where you'll find evidence."

He sounded friendly, Sam thought, but firm.

"I'll call you if they turn up back at the ranch," Mannix said, then started toward the Hummer.

"You do that," Sheriff Ballard said, then stood watching as Mannix drove the vehicle carelessly to the highway.

Once they were back in the truck, Sheriff Ballard radioed his office to tell Linc Slocum to stick around River Bend Ranch. After that, they drove in silence.

When Sam and the sheriff drove into the ranch yard, Sam saw the white curtain on the kitchen window pulled back.

Whoever was looking would notice they didn't have a horse trailer hooked on behind.

Gram held open the kitchen door and Jen stood behind her. Dad, Brynna, Mikki, and Gina sat at the kitchen table, watching expectantly as Sam walked inside. Linc sat there, too, but he barely glanced up.

"The horses were gone," Sam said.

Jen's hands went up to cover her eyes. Then, after a loud exhalation, her arms dropped to her sides and she returned to sit at the table along with the others.

"That's a shame," Brynna said.

Sam wanted nothing more than to climb the stairs to her room, pull the covers over her head, and pretend this day had all been a bad dream.

"We're just finishing a fried chicken dinner," Gram said, and only then did Sam notice the scent of Gram's buttermilk batter. "There's plenty left for you, Sam. And Sheriff, we'd love to have you join us. It's the least we can do after you taking so much time and trouble."

Shouldn't Linc be the one saying that? Sam let out a heavy sigh, but her tight chest felt no better for it.

"No, though I do thank you," Sheriff Ballard. He, too, waited for some reaction from Linc. "I should probably be getting back to town."

In a moment of silence, Linc rubbed his napkin across his lips and met the sheriff's gaze.

"You don't know what you're missing," Linc chuckled. He rocked his chair back on two legs and patted his belly.

"Put all four legs of that chair on the floor," Gram snapped.

Everyone at the table looked shocked. Gram had reprimanded Linc Slocum as if he were a kid.

Sam felt a cranky spurt of satisfaction.

He shouldn't act like one if he doesn't want to be treated like one, Sam thought.

"Sorry, Grace," Linc said as he complied.

Despite the sheriff's refusal, Sam noticed Gram had loaded two plates with chicken, mashed potatoes, and green beans.

Linc didn't seem interested in anything except the two biscuits left in the bread basket.

He eyed Sam with a raised eyebrow.

There was something kind of warped in the way he silently encouraged her to give permission for him to have hers.

Fat chance, Sam thought, but what she said before she even settled in her chair was, "Please pass the biscuits."

Chapter Nine ❧

"So the horses were just gone?" Jen asked, after Sam had eaten a few bites of dinner.

Sam noticed Jen covered her lips right after asking, as if the subject were too awful to discuss. Jen understood the horses' danger, and she was sharing the blame.

Linc Slocum didn't seem to. He swallowed a bite of chicken and gave Sam a smirk.

"And I suppose you know nothin' more about their disappearance than a hog knows about a sidesaddle," Linc said finally.

"I don't," Sam said. She was too tired and heartsick to fight, so she took a sip of milk before adding,

"The last time I saw Hotspot and Shy Boots, they were in that corral."

Linc shook his head with a snicker.

Sam was pretty sure it was the laugh that pushed Dad to the edge of his patience.

"Linc . . ." Dad began. He looked down as if addressing his plate, but Sam saw his knuckles were white from holding his fork so tightly. "Neighborliness has limits. If Sam says she doesn't know what's become of those horses, she doesn't."

"And you still haven't talked with your son," Sheriff Ballard pointed out as he took a bite of mashed potatoes.

"As a matter of fact, I have," Linc said. "Got him on his cell phone, which is why, and I hope you'll pardon me, Wyatt, but I've got to say it straight out, I'm convinced Samantha knows what's happened. Ryan told me she's the only one who knew where those Appaloosas were, and she promised to take care of them while he was gone."

"He told me—no, he *promised* me—he'd be back before nightfall!" Sam yelped.

Ryan was lying.

Her anger built as she thought of Ryan in San Francisco, a city she loved. She imagined him eating freshly caught crab and warm sourdough bread on Fisherman's Wharf. Or maybe he was sipping jasmine tea and breaking open a fortune cookie in Chinatown while she worried over the colt he claimed to care about.

"Give me his cell phone number," she told Linc, "and I'll find out what's really going on."

"I don't think so, young lady," Linc said.

Jen jabbed Sam with her elbow.

"Ow!" Sam said, frowning at her friend.

"Sorry," Jen said, but Sam could tell she wasn't. Her eyes were hinting at a secret.

"Sam's been home since two o'clock, Linc," Gram said. "Ryan dropped her off just before Jen arrived. Sam didn't have a chance to go anywhere."

"Sam didn't take the horses out of there," the sheriff said. "Unless she's taught herself to drive."

"That so?" Dad asked.

"Most likely," the sheriff said.

Sam was surprised, but heartened, when both Mikki and Gina gave her a thumbs-up and said, "Yeah!"

It was cool that they were on her side, Sam thought, remembering how Sheriff Ballard had bent to play his flashlight beam over the dirt before they even started up the hill. He must have been looking for tire tracks.

That let her off the hook, in one way, but her feelings were still all snarled up. Neither she nor the Phantom were directly to blame for the horses' disappearance. But she'd put Hotspot and Shy Boots in a place where they had no protection against thieves.

"Should I expect you to come into my office and file a report?" the sheriff asked Linc.

"Why wouldn't I?" Linc demanded.

"Just asking," Sheriff Ballard said.

"Do you still hang horse thieves out here?" Gina asked with a totally fake guffaw.

Sam winced. Gina had rotten judgment, but Sheriff Ballard just gave her a quick frown.

"We don't even catch most of them," he told her. "But we've got a good start on this one. Linc, you might want to get on the phone to Duke Fairchild at Mineral Auction Yards, first thing tomorrow morning."

Sam shivered and her eyes met Dad's. The last time they'd been at the auction yards, she and Dad had rescued Tinkerbell, a giant mustang who'd nearly been sold for slaughter.

It wasn't unusual for ranchers to bring aged saddle horses, or other animals they considered useless, to Mineral Auction Yards.

With nightmarish clarity, Sam remembered a man named Baldy. With his clipboard and calculator, he'd reduced each horse to its price per pound and decided whether to purchase it for the Dagdown Packing Company.

"Hotspot's a valuable horse," Sam said. "No one would sell her for—you know."

"The 'criminal genius' pretty much exists only on TV and in the movies," Sheriff Ballard said.

Gina made a soft noise of protest, but no one seemed to hear.

"I'm not saying it would happen, but it could. By the pound, those Appaloosas would sell for at least five hundred dollars," Sheriff Ballard said. "A thief could make a tidy profit for a few hours' work."

"That's awful," Jen said. "Do you think, by calling Mr. Fairchild, we can keep it from happening?"

We, Sam thought, smiling.

This was another reason Jen was her best friend. She'd already taken on the task of finding the horses. Sam guessed she could forgive her for that jab in the ribs.

"Duke keeps an eye on the stock coming into his place," Dad was saying. "He's a good businessman and sure doesn't want the publicity of selling a stolen horse."

"He told me he's especially careful accepting animals that arrive just minutes before the sales," Brynna said. "Most cattle and horse thieves give owners or neighbors as little time as possible to recognize stolen animals."

"Who wouldn't recognize their own horse?" Mikki asked.

Sheriff Ballard glanced pointedly at Linc, but Linc didn't notice. He was busy watching Gram arrange cookies on a platter.

"Horses can be disguised with hair dye," Brynna told Mikki. "Sometimes they'll trim manes and tails, too. At a glance, the horse might look like a completely different animal."

"There's more I can do, Linc," Sheriff Ballard said, thoughtfully, "if Hotspot is valued at more than $750."

The mention of money snagged Linc's attention away from Gram's cookies.

"You bet your boots, she is," Linc insisted. "Every animal on my place is! Except for that colt and Kitty, the mare I bought from—" He jerked his thumb toward Dad, and Sam felt herself grow hot with anger. He was talking about the Phantom's mother. "—they all have the finest bloodlines. Why, I was tellin' Karl just the other day that I've got millions of dollars tied up in my Brahmas, my Dutch Belted cattle, that Morgan of Rachel's, my saddlebreds, Quarter Horses, and that Thoroughbred—what's his name?"

He looked to Jen for the answer.

"Sky Ranger," she told him.

"Right, Sky Ranger. And I almost forgot those ponies from the Shetland Islands. They're worth more than all the others put together."

"Those shaggy little ponies?" Gram asked, then tsked her tongue.

"Abso-darn-lutely," Linc said. "They have their own insurance policy. And was it pricey? Whoo-ey, I just guess it was."

"The point of my question," the sheriff said, moving his hand in a rewinding motion, "was to establish that if they were stolen and valued over $750, the crime would be a felony," Sheriff Ballard said. "Since it is, I'll contact other law enforcement agencies. . . ."

Sam watched Linc as the sheriff and Brynna added up all the agencies they could turn to for help.

"The city police in Reno," Brynna said, thinking aloud, "and sheriffs' departments in the adjoining counties?"

"You bet," Sheriff Ballard said.

Sam was disappointed when Linc didn't seem a bit edgy. He didn't appear worried for himself or Ryan or the horses. His eyes didn't shift with uneasiness—they just kept darting toward the plate of cookies.

"Of course we'll keep watch among the wild horse herds," Brynna said. "Just in case."

"I'd like that done straight away," Linc said.

"So would I, but the federal government didn't figure the cost of putting up a helicopter to look for your lost Appaloosas into BLM's budget," Brynna said.

Linc crossed his arms and glared at Brynna. "I'm not joking," he said.

"And neither am I," Brynna said.

When Dad raised a hand to cover a cough, Sam was pretty sure he was trying to hide a smile.

"To tell you the truth, there's not much interest in this sort of case," the sheriff said. "Because evidence is hard to gather."

"Wouldn't someone need Hotspot's papers to get

the amount she's worth?" Jen asked.

"Papers can be forged," Sheriff Ballard said. "And some folks don't ask questions if they think they're getting a good deal." He was quiet for a minute, then turned to Sam with a smile. "But I know how I'd feel if someone made off with Jinx, so I'll do what I can."

"Thanks," Linc said idly. "Karl said he'd get on the Internet, too. He's a genius with computers."

I knew he looked like a computer nerd, Sam thought, and gave a satisfied nod.

"That's a good idea," the sheriff said, "and it wouldn't hurt if you put some flyers into local feed stores, at rodeos—anywhere people pay attention to horses."

"We could help," Brynna said suddenly.

"Help what?" Linc asked, but Brynna's gaze swept over Sam, Jen, Mikki, and Gina, and she smiled.

"Making phone calls and flyers would give us an extra project for the evenings, when we're not riding," Brynna said.

"Yeah," Sam agreed. "Like we did last time, tracking down the freeze brand on Jinx."

"That'd be cool," Mikki said.

When Gina nodded with a sly smile, Sam and Jen met each other's eyes. They hardly knew the girl, but they could tell she was up to something.

"Now, you ladies just leave it to the experts," Slocum said.

"Brynna is an expert," Sam snapped.

Linc must have felt Dad's glare, because he conceded, "You're right. I don't see how that could hurt.

"Time for me to go, I guess," Linc said as he pushed his chair away from he table. Standing slowly, he gazed toward the cookies Gram had yet to serve.

"Keep in touch, Linc," Sheriff Ballard said. "If you hear anything more from your boy, or if the horses happen to show up on their own—"

"Yeah, sorry to trouble you all," Linc said. "Thanks for the meal, Grace. I wish I could lure you away to cook for me. I swear, you do a much better job than that Coley woman."

Linc couldn't open his mouth without offending someone, Sam thought. He had to know "that Coley woman" was Helen Coley, one of Gram's best friends.

"I've got plenty to do right where I am," Gram said pleasantly.

As soon as the door closed behind Linc Slocum, Brynna sighed.

"There's no way in the world he'll go to any trouble for those horses. He'll just file an insurance claim and forget about them." Brynna turned to Jen, Mikki, and Gina. "Sorry to be so blunt, girls, but it's the truth."

"Probably so," Sheriff Ballard said.

"But Ryan loves those horses," Jen protested. Then, when she caught everyone looking at her, she pushed aside her affection for Ryan and added,

"Okay, I admit it doesn't look like it, but do you know what I think?"

The kitchen quiet was broken only by the sound of the grandfather clock in the living room, bonging seven.

"What do you think?" Sam asked finally.

"Ryan trusted you to do what was best for the horses. He knew you wouldn't leave them up there all night. He knew you'd find a way to go up and get them, even if you got in trouble."

Jen sounded so sincere, no one said anything.

Sheriff Ballard's hard eyes flicked to Sam's, though, and after he stood and thanked the Forsters for their hospitality, he nodded her way.

"Remember what I told you, Sam? I want you to think on it."

No one asked what the sheriff meant, though Sam could tell they were curious.

Sheriff Ballard might have a point.

Doing the wrong things for the right reasons was pretty much the story of her life.

After the dinner dishes were cleared, Brynna said that the girls could go settle into the bunkhouse. She wanted to get to bed early, so she'd be organized and alert for her five-thirty meeting with Sam and Jen.

"Couldn't we take turns showing up for that meeting?" Sam asked. It sounded like a great idea to her.

"As long as you don't mind taking turns when

HARP issues paychecks," Brynna said with a bright grin.

The girls groaned. That wasn't going to happen.

As they walked toward the bunkhouse, they rubbed goose bumps from their arms and gazed up at a blue-black sky studded with silver stars.

"It's a gorgeous sky," Gina said, tilting her head back as far as it would go as she kept walking. "But what happened to the whole desert thing? I'm freezing!"

"You're not," Jen said sensibly. "It must be forty degrees."

"Practically tropical," Sam said, but the joke ached. Where was Shy Boots? She feared the delicate colt wouldn't last long out in the cold.

"Still!" Mikki insisted. "It doesn't feel like a desert."

"It's the high desert," Jen explained. "We're at about fifty-five hundred feet elevation. You don't see any palm trees and camels, right? That's because it snows!"

"But not in summer," Gina said, purposely chattering her teeth together.

"I don't know," Jen said thoughtfully.

"It doesn't," Sam assured them.

"Actually I believe there's been snow in every month of the year," Jen said.

"In July?" Sam asked, and even as she said it, her smile faded. Could Hotspot protect her foal from the cold?

"I'll have to check," Jen said.

Once they reached the bunkhouse, Mikki and Gina crowded ahead to pick their bunk beds from those not already claimed by Sam and Jen. Sam motioned for Jen to stay outside.

"You guys go ahead and unpack," Sam called after Mikki and Gina. "We'll be right in." As the door closed, she asked, "What were you poking me for?"

"I have Ryan's cell phone number."

"You do? Why didn't you say so inside where there's a phone?"

"Because, if I know anything about Ryan, he won't answer his phone if he sees it's you calling."

"So you call and leave a message and ask him —"

"Nope, I'd be too understanding. I know," Jen said, holding up both hands to fend off Sam's glare. "I shouldn't be, but you'll make him feel guiltier."

"He *should* feel guilty!"

"Right, and once he does, he'll also start worrying about the horses. If you call him tomorrow or the next day, I bet he'll answer."

"By then, those horses could be anywhere," Sam said. "I'm not convinced this will work, Jen."

"Neither am I," Jen said. "On the other hand, what else have we got?"

"Good point," Sam said, and together, they walked into the bunkhouse.

* * *

Mikki and Gina were already piling toothpaste, hair gel, a clutter of hair ties, and other things in cubbies, making themselves at home.

Sam's spirits lifted at the sight. When her thoughts veered back to Hotspot and Shy Boots, she reminded herself that horses had survived in the wild for a million generations, and they wouldn't freeze in July.

The girls were jostling for space at the single sink, ready to brush their teeth, when Mikki asked, "So, hey, did you do it?"

"Do what?" Sam asked.

"Steal those horses."

Protests crowded Sam's mind, dizzying her, as Mikki added, "Not that I think it was a bad idea. I mean, he's a jerk. And if he planned to kill a foal, he doesn't deserve to have it. I think it's kind of cool, actually, but it really doesn't seem like you."

By the time Mikki took a breath, Sam's amazement had turned to anger.

"That's because it *isn't* like me. Yeah, I helped Ryan hide the horses, but I don't know where they are now."

Mikki and Gina looked at each other with surprise.

"Really?" Gina asked

"Of course, *really*!" Sam shouted. Her hand trembled so much, she had to tighten her grip on her toothbrush to keep from dropping it.

"You don't have to sound all mad!" Gina said.

Sam squeezed a huge glob of toothpaste on her brush and attacked her teeth.

Staring in the mirror, Sam blinked at Jen's acid-green nightshirt and loosened hair.

"Why shouldn't she sound mad? Sam doesn't steal," Jen snapped. Then Jen touched Sam's arm. "Hey, keep that up and you can say *adios* to your tooth enamel."

Sam coughed, choking on laughter and tooth-paste. Jen was such a good friend.

"Look," Sam said, once she'd recaptured her breath and rinsed her toothbrush, "I want to know where those horses are as much as—*more* than—Linc Slocum does!"

"If that's really true—" Gina began.

"It is!" Sam and Jen insisted, loudly and together.

"—I may be able to help you out." Gina rubbed her palms together, and Mikki rolled her eyes.

"Oh, right," Mikki said. "The world-famous seventh-grade livestock psychic from Commerce City, California, knows all and tells all!"

"I'm not exactly a psychic," Gina admitted. "But haven't you ever heard the expression 'it takes a thief to catch a thief'?"

Chapter Ten ౷

"**W**e're late," Jen moaned the next morning. "My first meeting on my first week working for HARP and I'm late."

It didn't feel late, Sam thought. The ranch yard lay gray and quiet. The rooster hadn't crowed yet.

Besides, it had taken Sam a long time to fall asleep. Last night she'd thought for hours, trying to figure out who had a motive to steal the Appaloosas.

Ryan's motive would be hiding the horses from his father. But they'd already been hidden.

Linc's motive could be getting rid of Shy Boots. But where was Hotspot? And Linc could already do what he liked with the horses, because they belonged to him. Why would he go to the trouble of moving them from the box canyon corral and away from Gold Dust Ranch?

Sam supposed her soft heart counted as a motivating factor, but she knew she hadn't stolen the horses.

Besides, she'd thought, as she'd turned her pillow over and pounded it for the last time last night, all three of them had alibis. It had to be someone else.

Now, Sam yawned as she eased the bunkhouse door closed, trying not to wake Mikki and Gina.

"Have you got the flyer?" Jen asked.

"Yeah," she whispered loudly, then took long strides to catch up with her friend.

Holding the flyer carefully so it wouldn't wrinkle, Sam wondered where Hotspot and her colt had spent the night, then told her brain to focus.

Last night, she and the other girls had combined Gina's suggestions with Sheriff Ballard's and designed a brochure to alert people to the danger of horse thieves, and seek information about Hotspot and Shy Boots. Right this minute, she couldn't do anything but see if Brynna thought it would help.

Falling into step with Jen, Sam glanced at her watch.

"We're not very late," she said. "It's only 5:33. I'll be surprised if Brynna's in the kitchen yet."

"But look." Jen pointed at the hitching rail.

Witch, Jake's black Quarter Horse mare, stood tethered there.

That's it, Sam thought. She had to get Jake up to the box canyon. He'd be able to read all the signs the horse thief had left behind.

Witch flattened her ears as Sam and Jen approached.

"How is it," Jen said through a yawn, "that Jake can gentle every horse he touches, except his own?"

"She never gives him a bit of trouble," Sam said. From habit, she stomped the dirt off her boots on the porch before going inside.

Sam smelled sausage frying and heard dough slam against Gram's breadboard as she and Jen came into the kitchen. After the counselors' early-morning meeting with Brynna, they'd rouse the girls and all have a big breakfast together.

Jake sat with both forearms on the kitchen table, hands overlapped where they met. He stared down into a cup of hot chocolate as if reading a crystal ball. His well-worn green-and-black plaid flannel shirt was open over a white T-shirt. As usual, his clothes smelled as if they'd just come out of the dryer, and his black hair, tied at his nape with a leather string, was still damp from the shower.

Sam tugged at the hem of her rumpled sweatshirt, and pushed her hair behind her ears.

"Were you just born to get up early?" she asked him.

Jake sat up straight. He lifted his cup for a drink, then looked at Sam across the brim.

Was he formulating a great answer? Sam wondered.

"Don't mind it," he said.

"Good morning," Gram greeted the girls, handing them each a mug of hot chocolate. "I'm sure Brynna will be down in a minute." Gram pointed up. Sam looked. She saw only ceiling, but she heard Brynna's feet scurrying overhead.

Slumped into chairs around the kitchen table, the three counselors waited in silence. Jake never had much to say. Jen turned half away and her fingers flew as she rebuttoned the fuchsia shirt she'd donned in the cabin's darkness. Sam wondered what Brynna would think of Gina's useful, if illegal, expertise.

"Sorry to be late," Brynna said as she strode into the room. Dressed in a khaki uniform with her hair tucked into a neat French braid, Brynna looked ready for the day, but her freckles stood out like sand on her pale cheeks.

"I may be getting a touch of the flu," she said, shaking her head "no" as Gram offered her coffee. "Which makes it even more important that this meeting is productive."

"Got it," Jen said.

As Brynna opened the folder she carried, Jen shifted around to pull a small notebook from her jeans pocket. Then she flipped the notebook open and Sam saw a carefully lettered list.

Another reason she earns straight As and I get mostly

Bad, Sam thought. Jen was so organized.

"I know we've discussed the schedule, but let's cover it one more time," Brynna said. "Jake, each morning you'll work one-on-one with Mikki and Dark Sunshine in the barn corral." Brynna glanced up to see Jake nod, then turned to Sam and Jen.

"At the same time, you two will have Gina working with Popcorn, starting with grooming, working through haltering, saddling, bridling, and finally riding. One instructs, the other models the task with another horse, okay?"

"Just what we planned," Jen said before Sam could answer.

"After lunch, Jake will instruct Mikki on riding Popcorn, while Jen demonstrates on Penny—" Brynna broke off to shake her index finger at Jen. "You be nice to my horse, understand? And stay alert. She may be blind, but she knows the second your attention wanders."

"I'm excited to be riding her," Jen said. "And I'm flattered that you're trusting me with her."

"At the same time, Sam, you and Gina will be working with Tempest, right?" Brynna made a quick swipe at the perspiration on her forehead.

Though the kitchen was warm, it wasn't hot. Brynna must really be sick.

"Any questions about the schedule?" Brynna looked up as they all shook their heads. Then she met Sam's eyes and gave her hand a squeeze. "I'm fine," she said. "Nothing for you to frown over.

"I'll be at Willow Springs every day, so if something's not working out, tell me and we'll switch the schedule around. Jake, that goes double for you."

Jake's brown eyes widened a little.

"You and Wyatt are so alike," she said in a joking tone. "You think you have to tough things out. That may be true on the range, but not here. You're not doing anyone a favor by keeping problems to yourself."

Sam felt a surge of appreciation for Brynna. Her stepmother had Jake sized up, all right.

Brynna held Jake's gaze until he said, "Okay."

Brynna turned to a green sheet in her folder. "About the girls . . . I can tell you that Gina—"

"—is proud of being a burglar?" Sam interrupted.

"It seems that way, doesn't it?" Brynna said. "Actually, she only started acting up when her mother remarried. Apparently when the stepfather moved into their house, Gina's grades dipped. She quit the softball team and stopped e-mailing her cousin in Colorado, the one who owns horses. Gina had pretty much cut herself off from her friends and all the things she liked and allowed her class performance to nosedive by the time her mom noticed."

Sam crossed her arms. "How did she go from that to robbing people?"

"Do I detect a lack of sympathy for Gina?" Brynna asked.

"Yes. I mean, no, but you and Dad got married and I didn't fall apart."

Brynna drew in a breath. She stared at her fingertips, slowly matching them together.

What a stupid thing to say, Sam thought, *especially in front of Jen and Jake, when Brynna's feeling sick*. But it was the truth.

Instead of snapping at her for acting superior, Brynna rested her palms on the kitchen table and gave Sam a smile.

"We have done pretty well, haven't we? But you can't see through the walls of other people's houses, Sam. Whatever went on in Gina's home, she couldn't cope with it like you could."

She didn't have you, Dad, and Gram to help her, Sam thought. But that was too sappy to admit.

"Okay," Sam said, and Brynna turned back to her notes.

"Gina started her baseball burglaries—"

"Which she's described to us in great detail," Jen interrupted. "And Jake, don't feel left out. She'll entertain you with her adventures about five minutes after she meets you."

Jake lifted one shoulder in a shrug as Brynna rushed on.

"—after her parents had a baby. The psychologist's evaluation says since Gina felt uncomfortable in her own home, she gave in to a compulsion to make other people feel the same way.

"So what kind of problems can we expect from her?" Brynna asked. She closed the folder and ticked them off on her fingers. "Lots of bids for attention — good attention, bad attention, attempts that will be both annoying and endearing."

Sam wondered which category last night's offer fell into. Gina wanted to catch the thief who'd stolen Hotspot and Shy Boots. That was good. But her help had been inspired by her burglary skills. Was that an improvement, or just showing off? Sam would have asked Brynna, but her stepmother glanced at the kitchen clock, obviously in a rush to finish.

"How do we deal with these bids for attention? Try to give her credit for the good stuff and attempt to ignore the rest."

Brynna had turned to the next page of her notes when Jen said, "Show her."

"Show me what?" Brynna asked, facing Sam.

"You know how Sheriff Ballard was talking about making a flyer to let people know about the missing horses?"

"You couldn't have made one. Not already."

Pride zinged through Sam as Brynna took the sheet of paper that Sam scooted across the table.

"We all worked on it," Jen said.

But Brynna was already lost in reading it.

"I can't believe you got two new girls to collaborate with you on this the first night!"

Brynna rearranged her chair so that Jake could look at the flyer, too.

"It's just hand lettered," Jen said.

"Someone will have to type it, and print it out," Sam added.

Shaking her head at their modesty, Brynna looked up at Sam and Jen with shining eyes.

"If I could, I'd give you a raise," Brynna said, but Sam smiled when Brynna couldn't stop reading the flyer. Such concentration was as good as money.

Gina's input included a section they'd entitled "Preventing the Theft of Your Horse!" In it, they listed prevention techniques as simple as sturdy fences, watchdogs, light and alarm systems, and more complicated things like motion detectors.

Together, they'd written a section called "Once Your Horse Is Gone!" There, they listed the sheriff's suggestions about contacting law enforcement agencies, breed associations, feed stores, vets, rodeos, and farriers. One thing they'd all agreed on had been a large-print, underlined warning that horses could be sold at auction and processed into meat within twenty-four hours.

"Grace, come look at this," Brynna said to Gram, then glanced up at Jen and Sam. "I am amazed. Where did you get this last part, about keeping all of the important papers pertaining to your horse?"

"Bill of sale, breed registration, brand or tattoo

records, updated photographs . . ." Gram read over Brynna's shoulder.

"That was Jen's idea," Sam said.

"It's just common sense," Jen said, blushing. "I know Dad has it for the Kenworthy palominos."

"And Sam, I can tell you did the illustrations," Brynna said, giving her an enthusiastic thumbs-up, for a horse she'd sketched to break up all the words. "What did you girls have in mind for the front?"

"We left it blank because we were hoping to get pictures of Hotspot and Shy Boots," Sam said. "And tell about their disappearance."

"I'll take care of that," Brynna said. She slipped the flyer into her folder. "Leave it to me, and as soon as I get that information, I'll make copies and get busy finding those horses.

"Pretty astonishing, isn't it, Jake?" Brynna said. "It's only Monday and they've already made those girls part of something special."

"Yep," Jake said with a nod.

Jake had been so still, Sam hadn't realized he was admiring their work, too.

Sam's spirits soared. Yesterday's rough start made today's praise even more welcome.

"Now, where was I?" Brynna said, lifting a sheet from her folder. "Right. Mikki.

"There's been no more shoplifting or running away. She's made up old class work and is passing this semester with a B average. She's made lots of progress and HARP can take most of the credit, since parental support is kind of . . ." Brynna wavered one hand back and forth.

"Inconsistent?" Jen suggested.

"Yes," Brynna said. "But Mikki will do fine. She loves Popcorn. He helped set her back on the right path. The only trouble I anticipate is a little jealousy over you, Sam."

Sam sat back in surprise. "Jealousy over me?"

"Jake was here before, but Jen wasn't and neither was Gina. As much as you and Mikki butted heads, she had you to herself."

"I don't know," Sam said dubiously. "We didn't like each other *before* she set the barn on fire with her stupid smoking," Sam said. "And that didn't make me like her more."

"But you like her now," Jen said, tipping her cup up to drain the last of her hot chocolate. "What changed?"

"I don't know," Sam said.

"Think it over," Brynna encouraged. "It might help with the other girls. Maybe even Gina."

In the thoughtful silence, they heard Jake's chair squeak as he shifted restlessly.

He froze, then studied his scraped knuckles.

"Enough discussion," Brynna said, snapping her folder closed. "You're off to a good start. Jen and Sam, why don't you make sure Gina and Mikki are up, and herd them on down for breakfast?"

"Can I call Sheriff Ballard first?" Sam asked.

"It's awfully early," Gram said as she jabbed a spatula into her skillet.

"I don't really expect him to be in his office," Sam said. "But if he is, don't you think he'll be working on finding Hotspot?"

Sam crossed her fingers. Unlikely as it was, she was actually hoping the sheriff had already found the horses.

"It would be more productive than calling Linc," Jen said.

"Go ahead," Brynna told Sam.

"I'll go get the girls," Jen offered. As she passed, she slipped a folded piece of paper into Sam's hand. "But you have to tell me what he said, right away."

"I promise," Sam said.

As she unfolded the slip of paper, Brynna came over to open the kitchen window.

"It's already heating up," Brynna said.

Sam didn't feel warmth, but Jake apparently agreed.

"Gonna take a walk," he said, nodding to Gram. "Be right back."

Sam didn't bother hiding Ryan's number. She'd have to get permission to make the phone call, anyway, if it turned out to be long distance.

"What's that?" Brynna asked, peering at the numbers Jen had written on the paper.

"Ryan Slocum's cell phone number."

For a few seconds, Brynna said nothing.

Gram stopped cooking, too.

"What's your plan?" Brynna asked.

"I don't have much of one," Sam admitted. "I'm just going to call and try to make him feel guilty."

Brynna and Gram both burst into laughter, but Sam had no clue what they found funny. Once their chuckles faded into smiles, Brynna asked, "What would be the point of that?"

"If he knows where the horses are, maybe he'll tell me. If he doesn't," Sam said with a big shrug, "I think he at least owes me an apology."

"Fair enough," Brynna said.

Sam tried Ryan's number first. She wasn't surprised when he didn't answer, but she left the message she and Jen had rehearsed: "Ryan, it's Sam. Hotspot and Shy Boots are gone. No one knows where they are. Call me and we'll put our heads together with Jen and Brynna and my dad and Sheriff Ballard. Call soon. If you wait, it's like you told me, 'you'll only have thrown away a chance to save them.'"

Sam hung up the phone, then realized the kitchen was unusually quiet.

Brynna applauded silently. "That ought to do it," she said.

"Gracious," Gram said. "You didn't give him much room to wiggle out of it."

"I hope it works," Sam said. She held up both

hands with fingers crossed, then overlapped her thumbs as well.

Brynna ran back upstairs to finish getting ready for work, and Sam opened the phone book and looked for Sheriff Ballard's telephone number.

As she scanned the dense columns of numbers, Jen and Jake's voices carried to her through the open window.

"You know, when Gina committed her burglaries, the only thing she stole was candy."

Jake grunted in response and Sam smiled. After her gloomy phone call to Ryan, hearing her best friends bicker really cheered her up.

"Candy," Jen repeated.

Jake wasn't getting whatever point Jen was trying to make.

"She stole candy," Jen said with forced patience. "As if she were trying to get back the childhood she lost with the creation of a new family."

Then Sam was pretty sure she heard Jake snort. And she was positive she heard him say, "Stick with horses, Kenworthy. At least they can't tell you that you're full of hot air."

Chapter Eleven ❧

Sam wasn't surprised Sheriff Ballard didn't answer his office phone. She listened to the recording that advised callers with emergencies what to do next.

"I guess this isn't an emergency," Sam said as she hung up and faced Gram. "But I can't stop thinking about Hotspot and Shy Boots."

"You can't do anything else, dear," Gram said. "The sheriff has his responsibility and you have yours."

The sheriff seemed convinced a wild stallion hadn't stolen them. A person had. But who?

Sam stared out the front window, but her eyes lost focus as she reviewed her suspect list from last night. Ryan, Linc, and her. But wait. Jen had known Ryan was planning to hide the horses, because she'd talked with him.

Had Ryan talked with anyone else?

And what about Linc? He'd sure noticed in a hurry that the Appaloosas were gone. Maybe Linc had suspected Ryan was up to something. Then Linc might have complained to Karl Mannix. That made Mannix a possible suspect, too.

Sam shook her head. The list just kept growing.

"Take your mind off those poor horses by setting the table, won't you?" Gram suggested.

Grumbling as she wouldn't in front of the HARP girls, Sam asked where everyone was supposed to sit.

"It will be crowded, but you'll figure it out, dear."

Although they'd left the leaf in the kitchen table from the last week of HARP, Brynna, Dad, Gram, Sam, Jen, Jake, Mikki, and Gina would have to sit elbow to elbow around the table.

Through the open window, Sam heard the girls talking as they crossed the yard. The kitchen door opened and slammed shut as Jake darted back inside ahead of them.

"What's wrong?" Sam asked.

"Nothin'."

"Then why are you in such a hurry?"

"I'm not," he said, but Sam could guess.

Jake's shyness was at its peak.

"How are you going to teach them if you can't

stay outside long enough for Jen to introduce you?"

Jake didn't answer. He watched her set the table as if he found knives and forks fascinating.

"Don't make me sit by one of 'em," he said.

"Jake," Sam started to laugh, and tell him to "cowboy up," but Jake's shyness was no joke. His pleading look made her give in. "Okay, but if you're not next to them, you'll have to face them across the table."

"Thanks," he said. But even when Brynna introduced him to Gina and asked if he remembered Mikki, even when Gina had to be cautioned to quit playing with her food and Jen talked about her summer school class, Jake kept his eyes on his breakfast.

Sam sipped her orange juice and studied him.

It was hard to believe this was the same Jake who'd bossed her around for half her childhood, the same teasing Jake with mischievous mustang eyes.

Come to think of it, though, his confidence grew around horses. Just when she thought she'd figured out some key to Jake's personality, Dad spoke up.

"Heard about Slocum's horses?" he asked Jake.

He'd seen the flyer, of course, but Dad's question made Jake become alert. He quit contemplating his food—which was nearly gone anyway—and lively interest shone in his brown eyes.

"Yeah," Jake said.

He didn't seem to notice that his low voice stopped all other conversation.

"Did Sheriff Ballard call you to look at the crime scene?" Sam asked.

"No."

"You've got to go look," Sam said. "There's tire tracks where we left the trailer, and the trailer had been messed with. I just know it. The latch was stubborn and Ryan had to lean down on it to make it close. And up in the box canyon—" When Sam snatched a breath, Brynna cut in.

"I'm not sure you can call it a crime scene, Sam. The sheriff didn't seem to think so."

"Wait," Mikki said. "I know how to tell." Mikki had slept her blond hair into a woodpecker crest, but her kelly green T-shirt made her look bright and awake. "Did he put up yellow crime scene tape like they do on television?"

"No," Sam conceded. "But something happened there and Jake is a really great tracker. He can see things in the dirt that are just invisible to other people."

Mikki and Gina studied Jake with new interest. Jake's glare told Sam he didn't appreciate the spotlight she'd thrown on him.

"Anyway, Sheriff Ballard *should* have asked you to look," she told Jake.

Ignoring her, Jake returned to staring at his plate.

Jen's exasperated sigh told Sam that she was

thinking the same thing. Horses had better be the key to opening Jake up, or it was going to be a very long week.

Brynna started out the door for work at Willow Springs Wild Horse Center before the girls had finished breakfast.

"I'm going to get started on this," she said, brandishing the flyer as if it had restored her energy. "With luck, we'll be able to hand some out tonight."

"You still thinkin' about goin' down to that preview night at the carnival?" Dad asked.

Sam didn't know what preview night at the carnival was, but it sounded fun and Brynna's smile was so brilliant, Sam knew her stepmother was feeling herself again.

"That's my plan," Brynna said. "Grace, don't even think about making dinner. We're going out!"

"We are?" Sam asked.

"You deserve a reward for starting work so early," Brynna answered. "Besides, last night I didn't feel too well, so I was sort of a party pooper. Tonight will be different. I promise."

Brynna was already pulling away in her white government truck as the girls left the house.

They'd just stepped onto the front porch when Popcorn's neigh floated over to them.

"Look at him," Mikki said. "He's so beautiful."

"I get to work with him first, right?" Gina asked.

Mikki stopped as if the question had hit her like a bucket of cold water. Glancing at Gina, Sam saw that the other girl wasn't trying to be mean. She'd just used that fact to grab everyone's attention.

"Right, Gina," Sam told her. "And it'll be tough brushing the grass marks off his coat, but you'll do it."

Jen must have noticed what was going on, too.

"Why don't you go catch him and bring him in," Jen suggested to Mikki.

"Me?" Mikki touched her chest. Her expression flickered between excitement and fear.

"Sure," Sam encouraged her. "You've done it before."

Ace had come to the fence, too. Together the albino and bay trotted a few steps off, but their ears pricked toward the group, ready for something to happen.

"Do you think he'll remember me?" Mikki asked.

"I don't know," Sam admitted. "Jake, what do you think?"

"Might," Jake said.

To Sam's surprise, Mikki took the single word as encouragement.

"Okay," Mikki said. "I'll do it."

Jen and the girls set off for the barn to get halters, lead ropes, and plastic buckets full of grooming supplies. When Jake started to follow, Sam grabbed his sleeve.

"We have to find the Appaloosas," Sam told him,

then braced herself for his refusal.

"I heard Linc tried to blame you," Jake said instead.

His jaw was set. Was he angry, or frustrated at the stupid accusation?

"He did. And even though the sheriff tried to talk him out of it, I—"

I'm still to blame. Those horses shouldn't have been up there and they wouldn't have been up there if I hadn't shown him the way, Sam thought.

That's what Sam wanted to say, but she knew the tears crowding her eyes would spill over if she did. So she just stopped talking.

"Don't take it so hard, Brat. They'll turn up."

Jake's understanding made Sam feel even sorrier for herself.

"And that guy Karl Mannix who works for Linc," she went on, "have you met him? He'll creep you out, for sure. Don't smirk, Jake. He will."

"I can feel the hair standin' up on the back of my neck already," Jake said with a straight face.

"I bet you"—Sam stalled, pointing an index finger at Jake and trying to think of something she wanted to win from him—"I bet you a cotton candy at the Fourth of July carnival that he'll give you the creeps."

"I'll risk it," Jake said, shaking her hand in agreement.

"Anyway," Sam went on, "I bet Mannix is the one

Ryan overheard his dad talking to about culling Shy Boots. What is *culling*, anyway?"

Jake shifted his jaw to one side, looking thoughtful.

"Lot of times, it's weeding out animals that don't fit in with your breeding program. Puppies that are too small, horses with bad conformation. But are you sure that's what he said?"

"Ryan heard him on the phone," Sam said, but Jake's small shrug reminded her that Ryan didn't always tell the truth.

"Just as long as you know it makes no sense, putting down a colt with his bloodlines," Jake said, then fell silent.

Sam watched Jake think. Once his curiosity started, it was like an itch.

Oh yeah, Sam thought. They might be going up to the box canyon, after all.

Sam heard the others returning from the barn, but she didn't take her eyes off Jake.

Jake didn't like Ryan. Part of his dislike had to be jealousy, since Ryan could buy everything Jake worked so hard for. But part of it, Sam conceded, was instinct. Ryan was untrustworthy. Jake had seen that in their first meeting.

Jake shrugged as if trying to shake off a persistent thought.

"It'd make sense to check the wild herds. That Appy mare ran loose for a while. Might be she's thinking freedom looks good, now her foal's born."

Sam nodded, but she knew how to add a little irritation to his curiosity.

"Don't worry about that," she said. "Brynna said BLM would watch for them."

Jake gave a snort. "BLM won't take the time."

"Brynna said it's too expensive to put up a helicopter, but—"

"More likely, BLM won't bother, 'cause they're too busy tellin' ranchers what to do."

Confrontations between the federal agency and ranchers didn't happen every day, but the animosity between them was never far beneath the surface. More than once, Sam had even seen it between Dad and Brynna.

Sorry, Brynna, Sam apologized silently, but she could see her plan working. Jake was on the verge of thinking this was his own idea.

"I say we ride out and check a few herds ourselves," Jake suggested. "I just got a hunch."

"Great," Sam said instantly. "But what are we going to do about"—she broke off and gestured at Mikki and Gina—"working?"

"We don't work 'til five thirty," Jake pointed out.

"Not—" Sam's mind spun as she realized what he meant. "Jake, I'm not sure there's *oxygen* before five thirty in the morning."

He ignored her dismay.

"I'll talk to Brynna," Jake offered. "The sooner

the better. I'll ask about tomorrow."

Sam knew it was the right thing to do. Sheriff Ballard had said the first twenty-four hours after a disappearance were critical, so if they couldn't ride out today, early the next morning would be best.

"How early?" Sam asked, bracing herself.

Jake squinted. "An hour out, hour back, and no guarantee of what'll happen in between . . . I'd say we could leave at three and maybe have a chance of seein' something."

"Three o'clock in the morning!"

"You're right," Jake taunted, "I should probably go alone. Not like I can't recognize a papered Appy."

"Jake, what makes you think I'd let you go out to the Phantom's herd without me?"

"You're too lazy to get up."

"Play nicely, children," Jen interrupted as she arrived with Gina and Mikki.

Jake's teasing expression fell away and Sam sighed.

"Fine," she told him. "I'll sleep when I'm old."

"Sam?" Mikki's whisper cut through Sam's self-pity.

"I'm not sure I remember how to catch Popcorn." She lifted the halter, keeping her back to Jen and Gina.

"You've already got his attention," Sam said, and pointed.

From the center of the pasture, Popcorn's blue

eyes watched Mikki. He swished his tail, stamped a front hoof, but didn't look away.

Sam opened the gate and beckoned Mikki through.

"Just use his name, show him the sweet grain, and you're home free."

"Here goes nothing," Mikki said, and then she was walking through the pasture.

Mikki looked up at the sky. It was turning blue now, showing white cotton-ball clouds. Sam could tell there was no place else Mikki would rather be.

"Shake the grain can a little bit," Jen called to her. "Good, like that, and hold the halter down by your leg."

Sam couldn't tell if the gelding remembered Mikki, but he recognized kindness and rubbed his head against her in appreciation.

"She's flyin' now," Jake said.

He was right. Mikki's grin spread wide, plumping her cheeks so high, they almost closed her eyes.

"How's she doing, really?" Gina asked Sam.

"Perfect, so far," Sam answered, but then she heard Gina's pouty tone. "She's had experience. You'll be doing that soon, too."

"When?" Gina demanded.

"'Bout ten minutes from now," Jake said.

Gina turned to him, blinking in surprise, but Jake looked at Sam.

"Ten minutes sounds about right," she told Gina.

"We'll do it in the round corral."

"But I . . ." Gina searched for an excuse. For once, she had more attention than she wanted.

"Watch," Jake ordered. And Gina did.

Popcorn lowered his head as Mikki stopped in front of him. He lipped up the grain, trying to keep Ace from snatching any, but even when he finished, Popcorn remained there, head lowered for the halter.

Jen moved to the pasture gate, ready to open it as soon as Mikki returned.

The gelding bobbed his head, white mane flopping in eagerness.

"I don't get how she's going to catch him," Gina protested.

"She'll just slide the lead rope over his neck, behind his ears," Jake said. "Then, she'll hold it together under his throat . . ."

Jake paused. They all watched as Mikki caught the willing albino. Haltering him was a fumbling, awkward action, but she managed to slip the noseband past Popcorn's lips and nostrils, lift the straps up his cheeks, and buckle the halter into place.

Mikki stroked the albino's neck, and Popcorn's skin shivered.

"How many hands does that take?" Gina asked Jake, but it was Mikki who called out an answer.

"Three," she said. "But I've got him."

Sam and Jen laughed as Mikki, with a jaunty step, led Popcorn back toward the gate Jen was opening.

"Watch Ace," Sam cautioned.

Refusing to be left behind, the bay gelding bolted past Popcorn and Mikki. Jen used both hands to slam the gate closed, and Ace slid to a stop.

Then he gave a plaintive nicker in Sam's direction.

"My poor baby," Sam said, smooching as Ace tossed his black forelock to show the white star between his eyes. "He can come out, Jen."

"If you're sure," Jen said.

"Beggin' for trouble," Jake muttered.

"You think you know everything," Sam teased him.

Then, with a slam of horseflesh against wood, Ace came out bucking.

Chapter Twelve ❧

For an instant Sam was afraid she'd made a mistake.

Sunlight glinted on Ace's red-gold coat and highlighted his muscles, making him look every inch a mustang.

Jen helped Mikki lead Popcorn out of Ace's path and Sam turned to Gina.

"Careful," Sam cautioned her, but just as quickly as it had begun, Ace's burst of high spirits switched to curiosity as he spotted Gina.

With a snort and a tilt of his head, Ace walked toward the new girl.

"Are you okay with him checking you out?" Sam couldn't see Gina's face in the shade of her baseball cap, but the girl nodded.

Gina kept her feet braced apart as Ace sniffed her gray sweatshirt.

"He's mine," Sam said, coming to stand beside Gina. "And he's just introducing himself. Gina, this is Ace, the smartest, sweetest horse on River Bend Ranch."

When Sam planted a loud kiss on Ace's nose, Jake shook his head in disgust.

"I'll be in the corral," Jake said, and walked away.

When Gina raised a hand to pet Ace, Sam relaxed and turned her attention back to Jen and Mikki.

"You did great," Jen told Mikki. "How about giving Popcorn over to Sam, now, and following your"—Jen raised her voice so Jake would hear—"always gregarious teacher over to the barn corral."

As if she had to force each finger to part with the lead rope, Mikki surrendered Popcorn to Sam.

"He doesn't want to work with me, does he?" Mikki asked, staring after Jake.

"Of course he does," Sam said. "He's embarrassed because I got mushy with Ace."

"Just follow him," Jen told Mikki. "And don't be surprised if he gives Dark Sunshine more attention than he gives you."

"That's fine with me," Mikki said.

"I don't know," Gina said in a lazy voice. "I think Jake's kind of hot."

"Kind of *what*?" Jen's outburst made Ace snort

and Popcorn back away with rolling eyes.

Sam felt like doing the same.

"I'm outta here," Mikki said.

As Mikki hurried after Jake, Sam admired her good sense. Mikki was doing exactly what Brynna had suggested, ignoring Gina's bids for attention.

But gosh, couldn't Gina go five minutes without insisting everyone notice her?

First, Gina had made a point of rubbing it in that she'd work with Popcorn. Now, she'd made a stupid remark about Jake.

"Don't you think he's cute?" Gina asked. She pulled off her baseball cap and her green eyes watched for Sam's reaction.

Sam forced a smile, then shrugged.

"I've known him since I was born," she said, and then she and Jen made Gina buckle down to work.

In the round pen, Jen unhaltered Popcorn and instructed Gina in how to rehalter and groom the albino, while Sam demonstrated each task on Ace.

Every now and then, they heard Dark Sunshine's angry squeals from the barn corral. Once, they heard the sound of an equine body hitting the fence.

That time, Sam and Jen's eyes met.

The buckskin mare was a troubled animal. Though she was supposed to be part of the HARP program, she'd never quite fit in.

Midway through the morning, Sam glimpsed movement from the corner of her eye. Someone was watching through the rails of the round pen.

It was Gram.

Please let her have news about the lost horses, Sam thought. And then she turned to Jen.

"Go ahead," Jen said, seeing Gram.

"What about me?" Gina said. "Don't I get a break?"

Without answering, Sam slipped through the gate, closed it behind her, and took a deep breath, suddenly aware of how dusty it had been inside the corral.

"Has Ryan called?" Sam asked.

Gram shook her head. "I would have hollered for you if he had," Gram said, "but I did talk with Duke Fairchild. The good news is, he hasn't sold any Appaloosas. There hasn't been one at Mineral Auction Yards in months."

"Why don't I feel relieved?" Sam asked.

"Because we still don't know where Hotspot and her baby are," Gram said.

Sam wanted to get rid of this big iron horseshoe of guilt that was hanging around her neck, but that wouldn't happen until the horses were safe.

"I learned something else," Gram said. "According to Helen Coley, Karl Mannix has left town."

Sam closed her eyes as if she could block out this extra information. She'd never make a good detective. It was way too confusing.

"Then—wait," Sam said. "Can the sheriff go after him? Isn't that kind of suspicious?"

"I'm sure Heck Ballard will talk with Linc," Gram said.

"I mentioned it to him when he called back."

"Sheriff Ballard called back?" Sam asked.

"Yes, but he hasn't uncovered anything new, and with all the folks coming into town this weekend for the Fourth of July festivities, he's terribly busy."

Gram waggled the pencil she held between two fingers. Sam couldn't help noticing Gram had been doing all of the work that she'd encouraged Sam to leave to the sheriff.

"You've really been busy," Sam said.

"I like to help," Gram said. Then, seeing Sam notice the pencil, she skewered it through the tidy bun of her gray hair. "One more interesting thing," Gram said, frowning. "When I called Sterling Stables, they didn't know anything about all this."

"That doesn't make sense. Linc told us he'd called to see if Ryan had dropped off Hotspot. Didn't he?"

"All I know is, it would certainly simplify things if everyone told the truth." Gram gave a fierce nod. "Still, I talked with Katie Sterling and she offered to fax the sheriff a list of Appaloosa fanciers, in case he wanted to send a 'be on the lookout' bulletin.

"Yes, most of what Katie said was reassuring." Gram's voice slowed.

"Most?" Sam asked.

"Katie's read up on modern-day horse thieves," Gram said. "And it seems, sometimes, foals are just too much trouble. Thieves want easy-to-handle horses."

A mare with a foal was rarely easy to handle. Sam suppressed a shudder at what she knew was coming.

"To keep a mare settled down, they'll"—Gram paused, searching for the right word—"split up the mare and foal."

"And sell them separately?" Sam asked, but it took Gram too long to agree.

Sam felt sick. Gram hadn't been searching for the right word, just the kind word. Katie Sterling had suggested that Shy Boots might be killed.

Dad had driven into Alkali for chicken feed and Gram was leading Sweetheart around the ranch, giving the old mare some exercise, but she left lunch and a list of phone numbers in the kitchen.

Sam and Jen took turns eating sandwiches with Gina, Mikki, and Jake, and calling neighbors Gram hadn't gotten to yet.

Though everyone was sympathetic and mildly critical of Linc for not making his own phone calls, no one had seen the mare and foal.

"I talked with Grace this morning," Mrs. Allen said when Sam called the Blind Faith Mustang Sanctuary.

"I'm sorry to bother you again," Sam apologized.

"Don't be silly. I've spent my morning wondering what you've missed and I finally thought of something."

Ever since she'd taken in a herd of unadoptable mustangs, Mrs. Allen had become what Gram called a go-getter in everything.

"We'd love your suggestions," Sam said. She glanced over at Jen, who gave a thumbs-up gesture, and Mrs. Allen must have been feeling pretty excited herself, because Sam heard the old lady's Boston bull terriers yapping in the background.

"Shady dealings are conducted on the Internet." Mrs. Allen's tone was ominous.

"Yes," Sam said in what she hoped was an encouraging voice.

"I never go near computers myself, but from what I've read in the newspaper, the Internet is a hotbed of crime."

"You're probably right," Sam said.

"I daresay you could find a few unscrupulous horsemen who'd buy a mare and foal without asking for proper ownership papers. Those machines just seem to bring all sorts of creeps out of the woodwork."

Creeps like Karl Mannix, Sam thought. Linc had said Mannix was a computer genius.

But she'd lost track of what Mrs. Allen was prattling about.

". . . don't you, dear?"

Sam took a deep breath. Keeping up a conversation with Mrs. Allen was like riding a spirited horse. It was a bad idea to let your mind wander. But she had a fifty-fifty chance of answering the old lady's question correctly.

Sam crossed her fingers and answered, "I don't."

"Well, I'll try to be more to the point, but not too gruesome," Mrs. Allen said. "Someone could be holding the pair somewhere and fattening them up to sell for meat."

"That would be awful," Sam admitted.

"Truly awful, so if I were you, dear, I'd get your little band of bad girls working harder. You need to find those horses while they're still alive."

The afternoon went smoothly, and if Jake wasn't very talkative about how Dark Sunshine and Mikki had done together, that wasn't exactly a shock.

By the time Brynna arrived home, her morning energy had worn off. She leaned against the refrigerator, sipping a glass of orange juice as the girls celebrated the finished brochure.

"Look at this," Sam said to Mikki and Gina. "We're amazing!"

"I heard Linc was out of town," Gram said as she examined the perfect photograph of Hotspot on the front of the flyer. "Brynna, did Karl Mannix get this for you?"

"No. I didn't ask him," Brynna said. "For some

reason I remembered the mare came from the Spanish Moss Plantation in Florida. When I called and told them what I needed, they were only too happy to send me all they had on Hotspot."

"I have a list of where we should drop off flyers," Jen said, showing Brynna her little notebook.

"That's a long list," Brynna said. Her eyes swung to Dad as he came inside.

"You still feeling a little sick?" he asked.

"Tired," Brynna admitted. "But if I could grab a ten-minute nap before we started out, I'd be good as new."

"You go right along and do that," Gram encouraged her, and Brynna didn't have to be told twice.

Sam was retreating with the rest of the girls to get cleaned up for the trip to Darton when she noticed Dad and Jake talking by Dark Sunshine's corral.

"What's going on?" Jen asked Sam, as she noticed, too.

"I don't know, but I'll find out," Sam said.

"Are you ditching me with the girls again?" Jen said.

Sam froze, remembering how she'd asked Jen to wake the girls this morning while she called the sheriff, then to keep working with Gina while she stepped outside the round pen to talk with Gram. Now this.

"I'm sorry," Sam said.

"It was a joke, Sam," Jen assured her. "I think

this is really fun. I like not splitting duties with you."

"Honest?" Sam said, watching her friend closely.

"Cross my heart," Jen said with a quick gesture. "I may be a natural-born counselor."

"Okay," Sam said. "But I won't take my eyes off either of them when we get to preview night. I promise."

Chapter Thirteen ❧

Squatting and looking down at the dust instead of each other, Dad and Jake were talking like cowboys.

Dad used a twig to mark something on the ground and Sam decided they must be talking about riding out to look for the Appaloosas.

Should she approach casually, as if she'd just happened to mosey by? Or just stride right up and be honest about it?

Sam approached openly, but Dad and Jake didn't seem to notice. When she got close enough to hear their conversation, she was surprised how much it concerned her.

"I'd go alone," Jake muttered, "but havin' her will cut my approach time in half."

"Yep. She can call that stud to her like a lapdog. And she puts him in worse danger each time she does," Dad said.

Sam couldn't have felt worse if her heart had stopped beating.

"Go alone, Jake," Sam said as they both looked up.

"Brat—" Jake started.

"Honey," Dad interrupted, sighing. "Checking from a distance won't hurt that stallion. You'll be able to spot those Appaloosas from a mile away."

"No. You're right, Dad. If I wanted Blackie tame, I'd adopt him."

"Is that so?" Dad said.

Sam ignored Dad's faint smile and crossed her arms. She'd made this decision long ago.

"I want him free, Dad. Each time he doesn't run from me, he's more at risk from someone who wants to catch him," Sam said. "Maybe BLM wranglers could ride out there."

"Maybe," Dad said.

"Linc's just going to think I turned them loose anyway, so it's not going to change anything," Sam said.

She gazed through the fence rails at Tempest and Dark Sunshine, knowing how miserable she'd feel if they'd disappeared.

Her hands clenched in frustration. Someone had to go check the wild herds, and Jake was right. She could get him closer, sooner. But how close was too close? How many visits would make the Phantom too tame?

Sam was still watching the Phantom's filly when she heard the bunkhouse door open on a wave of chatter.

Dad noticed, too.

"Well, we'll talk about this a little later, 'cause here comes trouble if I've ever seen it. And whew." Dad made a loud sniff. "I can smell the perfume from here."

Mikki and Gina both wore white shorts with red shirts. Jen followed in fresh jeans and a blue-and-white blouse spangled with red stars.

Sam looked down at the riding clothes she'd worn all day. She didn't look a bit festive. She might have run to the house and changed if Brynna hadn't sauntered out to meet the other girls just then.

"Ready?" Brynna called toward the barn.

"Just about," Dad said.

Jake rubbed the back of his neck and swallowed. "Will you be needin' me to come along?" he asked.

"Naw," Dad said. "Best thing you can do is ride along home. We'll try to handle this wild bunch without you."

All four girls fit in the backseat of Gram's Buick, but barely, so it was Brynna who climbed out in Alkali, to leave flyers at Clara's coffee shop and the general store that was part of the gas station.

Making up for a day away from the HARP girls, Brynna had asked Mikki about her reunion with Popcorn, and Mikki was still explaining when they'd driven halfway to Darton.

Pinned between the car window and Gina, Sam felt the younger girl fidgeting.

Probably because Brynna's paying attention to Mikki, Sam thought. And probably, if she were a good HARP counselor, she'd talk with Gina, so she wouldn't act up for attention.

But Sam kept her eyes fixed on the passing scenery, hoping she'd see two chocolate-colored horses with Appaloosa spots.

"What are you doing?" Gina said, elbowing Sam. "Pouting because now you've got a criminal rep like the rest of us?"

"A criminal rep?" Jen asked before Sam could. "A reputation, you mean?"

"Yeah."

Sam didn't know how Gina's tone managed to imply Jen had no experience with real life, but it did.

Dad started to say something, but Brynna touched his arm and shook her head.

"Everyone has a reputation for something," Brynna said. "I hope I have one for being a fair boss and a decent biologist. Jen has a reputation for being a level-headed genius," Brynna joked. "And everyone knows Sam is a wild horse expert."

"You can try to brand someone with a bad reputation, but it don't necessarily take," Dad said.

They drove in silence for a few seconds before Gram, buckled into the front seat between Dad and Brynna, spoke up.

"The best words I ever heard about making your own reputation," Gram said, looking over her shoulder into the back seat, "is that you come into the world crying while everyone else is smiling at the miracle of you, and you should live your life so when you leave it, you're smiling, but everyone else is crying because the miracle of you is gone."

"That's so cool," Mikki said, but Gram's words of wisdom didn't lighten Sam's mood.

If even one person thought she was responsible for the horses' disappearance, she had to do something.

Driving toward the fairgrounds, they stopped at Crane Crossing Mall and left flyers at the Western wear and tack stores, so it was dusk by the time they arrived.

Climbing out of the car into the warm July evening, Sam felt the bustle of preview night at the carnival. The hum of excitement made it impossible to mope.

Sam strolled the fairgrounds with Jen on one side and Mikki on the other. Gina forged ahead as if she knew where she was going. Dad and Brynna lagged behind, holding hands.

Hammers pounded and power tools whined as rides that would be running Friday night were rolled down from trucks and rebuilt.

Vendors climbed ladders to hang red, white, and blue bunting. Service groups that would sell barbecued beef sandwiches and cotton candy later yelled back and forth, testing lights.

A woman wearing a gray canvas apron pulled coupons from her pouch-like pockets and urged them to visit the two things that were already running—a hotdog stand and the carousel.

Brynna bought corn dogs on sticks for everyone. They meandered around the fairgrounds, eating and handing out flyers while merry-go-round music followed them.

"Pretty cool," Mikki said.

"Pretty bor—" Gina broke off when Jen and Sam turned to glare at her. "Quiet."

"It's just a small-town carnival, and it's not even set up yet," Brynna said, almost agreeing. "But you could be back at the ranch, cleaning out the barn."

"Or washing dishes after Gram made some huge feast for dinner," Sam suggested.

"Okay, it's fun enough," Gina said, and even though she pulled her baseball cap down to hide her eyes, Sam heard the smile in her voice.

"Hey, check that out!" Mikki said, pointing.

PATTY'S PRONTO PETTING ZOO read the blue-and-white-striped awning that swooped up like a tent to shade an enclosure. CUTE, LOVEABLE, FRIENDLY, AND CLEAN said one banner. ANIMAL HANDLER ALWAYS READY TO ANSWER QUESTIONS said another.

Shy Boots was cute and loveable. What if—

Sam rushed to look inside, but the enclosure was empty.

"Too bad, there's nothing to pet," Jen said, joining in Sam's disappointment as she came to stand beside her.

Sam smiled at her friend, but she didn't share her one instant of crazy hope with Jen.

"Come back on the Fourth of July, and you'll see goats, sheep, pigs, and ducks."

Sam turned toward the new voice. A woman in jeans and a khaki shirt might have passed for a teenager, except for the gray in her brown braids and squint lines around her eyes.

"And over in the sitting area," the woman continued, "you'll be able to hold bunnies and guinea pigs."

"Hi," Sam said, studying the woman.

"Hi, I'm Patty." The woman pointed to the name on the awning. "And I even let big kids like you in, if you behave."

"Cool," Mikki said, as Patty gave them each a dollar-off coupon for the petting zoo.

Instead of looking at the coupon in her hand, Sam read the poster taped to the petting zoo's admission booth.

Patty apparently used her animals for children's birthday parties and Christmas nativity scenes, as well as fairs and carnivals.

Though one line of type said, "I love my animals and reserve the right to expel anyone from the petting pen," Sam felt wary.

"Where do you get your animals?" she asked.

Suspicion must have tinged her tone, because Patty looked startled.

"I mean, do you take pets that people don't want anymore?" Sam added.

"I only buy animals from reputable breeders, but there's no shortage of people trying to give me pets they've gotten sick of. I hope you're not one of them."

Patty's hands perched on her hips, and while Sam was deciding she liked this woman a lot, Brynna laughed.

"Hardly," Brynna said. "According to my husband, we're running a home for old chickens. We have two Rhode Island Red hens—"

"Three," Dad added.

"—that haven't laid eggs in over a year."

"My kinda folks, then," Patty said, nodding. "Some people have no loyalty to their animals, though, and it's hard to refuse, but I make precious few exceptions."

Sam felt guilty for thinking this nice woman might be in league with whoever had stolen Hotspot and Shy Boots.

That was just wishful thinking that didn't make sense, she decided. She wanted this search to be over.

Sam handed Patty one of the flyers, but the woman spared it only a glance before slipping it in her pocket.

"I do have two potbellied pigs," Patty said as Mikki and Gina investigated the zoo. "Some woman bought them for her husband, then divorced him and thought it would serve him right if she had Hamlet and Ophelia—that's what she named them—made into pork c-h-o-p-s."

Patty glanced around as if the pigs were nearby. And could spell.

"My only other exception is a pregnant burro who was captured in the desert outside Las Vegas. She won't be here Fourth of July, because she's due to foal any day."

"What's her name?" Mikki asked.

"Mistress Mayhem," Patty said grandly. "But I call her May, and despite her bossiness, she makes a lovely addition to a nativity scene."

"We'll look forward to seeing you on Friday," Brynna said. She glanced after Gina, who had walked on to watch the setup for a pitching booth. Milk bottles made of tin rolled everywhere, and Gina bent to help a man pick them up.

"I'm always here," Patty insisted as Sam looked back at her. "Where my animals are, that's where you'll find me! They're my family. My son hates it when I say that," Patty said as Sam waved good-bye.

Mikki decided to pass up a ride on the carousel.

"I'm a little sore," she admitted. "Just the idea of throwing a leg over one of those wooden horses makes me hurt."

"Well, I don't want to ride alone," Gina said. "But if that guy had his pitching booth open, I'd show you something."

"Could you win me a stuffed animal?" Mikki asked.

There was something sad about Gina's smile as she nodded. "I used to be really good at that."

After Sam and Jen passed out their remaining flyers, they all left for home.

Both HARP girls and Gram were dozing by the time the Buick passed the turnoff to Gold Dust Ranch.

"Do you think Linc's told Ryan that Karl Mannix took off?" Jen whispered to Sam.

"Do you think he'd care?" Sam asked, hoping Jen wouldn't get mad.

"I think he would," Jen said.

Brynna twisted in her seat, listening.

"Can we call him again when we get back to the house?" Jen asked Brynna.

"It's pretty late," Brynna said.

Sam and Jen stared at each other, even though they couldn't see each other's expressions in the dark car.

"It probably won't make any difference if we wait until morning to tell him that Mannix took off," Jen said.

Sam gazed into the desert darkness and hoped Jen was right.

Chapter Fourteen ❦

They'd just bumped across the bridge over the La Charla River and rolled into the ranch yard when Gram straightened in the front seat, suddenly awake.

"The barn light's on," she said.

"I see that. Looks like Pepper wants to have a word," Dad said.

What now? Sam thought. She stared toward the barn, trying to make out the shapes of Dark Sunshine and Tempest, but she only saw Pepper's shadow cross the bright square that was the barn door.

The cowboys—Pepper, Ross, and Dallas—were usually relaxing in their own bunkhouse by now, but Pepper stood where he knew Dad would park, waiting.

Pepper was lanky and young, an Idaho cowboy

nicknamed for his chili-pepper red hair. As the girls piled out of the car, he took a long stride toward Dad.

"Had a little trouble with one of them"—Pepper glanced at Sam and she had the feeling he amended what he'd been about to say—"wild horses. That white stallion."

Electricity might have jolted through every nerve in Sam's body. Trouble with the Phantom?

"What happened?" Sam pushed past the others to face Pepper.

"Everyone's okay." He used both hands to make a "settle-down" motion. "But Tank fell and scraped his knees bad, trying to get away."

Tank was a bald-faced Quarter Horse, usually ridden by Ross. The gelding was big—so big that Sam feared a fall would be more serious for him than for a smaller horse.

"Shall I call Dr. Scott?" Sam asked. The vet's number was posted next to the phone in the kitchen.

Lips pressed together in a straight line, Dad looked toward the barn, then shook his head. Sam knew what he was thinking. Tank was a valuable cow horse, but vet bills were expensive.

"Dallas patching him up?" Dad asked.

"Yeah. Looks like he'll be okay."

"Girls, you can go on and get ready for bed," Brynna said, but when none of them moved, she was too distracted to insist. "What happened with the stallion?"

"We saw some mustangs over by Aspen Creek, and Ross thought he spied an Appaloosa among 'em," Pepper said. "We were joggin' over to see, when that stud horse charged out of nowhere and ambushed us."

Sam shivered. Aspen Creek wasn't the Phantom's usual territory. Charging riders on horseback wasn't the way he usually behaved. But Pepper would recognize her horse.

"As soon as they got up—"

"I didn't even ask about Ross," Brynna said suddenly. "Is he all right?"

"Fine," Pepper said, nodding. "And we wanted to ride closer and see if he'd seen Slocum's mare, but Tank took the hide right off his knees and the way he was bleedin' we knew we needed to bring him on home slow. And it was getting toward dark."

"Sounds right to me," Dad said, watching as Gram and Brynna walked purposefully toward the barn. Then he turned to Jen and Sam. "Why don't you all get bedded down for the night. I'm going to call Linc and tell him the news."

All four girls returned to the bunkhouse. As she and Jen tried to ease the girls toward a peaceful sleep, Sam realized they were acting like real counselors.

Sam was brushing her teeth and wondering what Linc had said about Hotspot when she heard Brynna's hushed voice at the bunkhouse door.

Although Sam and Jen were both in nightgowns, Brynna motioned them outside.

"What's up?" Sam asked, ignoring Blaze as he sniffed loudly at her bare toes.

"Your dad and I have been talking," Brynna began.

"What did Linc say?" Jen interrupted. "Has he heard anything from Ryan?"

"Linc didn't seem concerned about Hotspot or the fact that he hasn't heard from Ryan," Brynna said.

"I'm shocked," Sam said sarcastically.

"And he told Wyatt that he and Karl Mannix parted on friendly terms."

A breeze chased through the ranch yard and Blaze pricked his ears up at the sound of a distant owl.

"Since Linc didn't seem inclined to do it, I left a message at Sheriff Ballard's office, just to let him know the mare might have been seen—"

"Everyone keeps saying 'the mare,'" Sam said. "Isn't Shy Boots with her?"

"Probably," Brynna said, then she yawned.

Sam studied her stepmother. She still looked a little pale. "You should get to bed," Sam said.

"What do you want us to do?" Jen asked.

Brynna considered them both with a grateful smile.

"Unfortunately, I have a teleconference with my boss in Washington, D.C., or I'd stay home tomorrow," Brynna said.

"We can handle everything here," Jen said.

"That's good, but Jen, I'm afraid I'm going to leave you shorthanded," Brynna said. "Even though it's not really our responsibility, Wyatt and I have decided Sam has the best chance of getting close enough to the Phantom's herd to see if Hotspot and Shy Boots really are there."

"I just don't . . ." Sam began, but she couldn't finish.

Sam felt as if a chalk line had been marked down the center of her heart. She didn't know whether to help the Appaloosas or the Phantom.

"Your dad told me you have qualms about going, and I think they're well-founded. Still, want to or not, you and Jake are nominated."

Cowgirl up, Sam thought.

"And," Brynna went on, "I've already called Jake and he'll be here in"—Brynna reached for Sam's wrist and turned it so she could see the face of her watch—"five hours."

Jen suddenly looked happier about her part of tomorrow's plan.

"Sweet dreams," Brynna said. She gave Jen a pat on the back and Sam a kiss on the cheek, then hurried back to the ranch house.

Three taps from a single fingertip against the bunkhouse door brought Sam awake in the darkness.

Jake was here.

Sam sat up and stared at her watch. It was already three o'clock.

She eased out of her bunk and stood listening, but no one stirred.

She'd gone to sleep wearing everything but her boots.

What time had Jake gotten out of bed to be here on time? Sam wondered as she tugged on the boots. And why hadn't she heard his truck rumble over the bridge and into the ranch yard?

Sam ran her fingers through her hair, grabbed her jacket and hat, then slipped outside.

She stood blinking in darkness. Where was Jake?

Thudding hooves and a questioning nicker told her he was in the ten-acre pasture, catching horses. She'd barely finished the thought when she saw him lead Ace and Nike through the faint beam of the front porch light.

Sam had known Jake wasn't going to take the time to load Witch and trailer her over this morning. She wondered what had made Jake pick Nike over the other River Bend horses, but it was too early to ask.

"Hi," she whispered.

"You were quick."

Sam smiled in the darkness. It was a small compliment, but it spurred her to work even faster to smooth on Ace's saddle blanket, heft her saddle onto his back, and rock it into place.

They were ready and swinging into their saddles

in the same moment, and not even Blaze had come out to investigate.

"Which way?" Sam asked.

They could ride through the ranch, past the barn, and up a trail to the ridgeline that ran behind River Bend and Three Ponies Ranch to reach Aspen Creek, but if they went the front way, they could scan the wild terrain for the Phantom's herd, and that was the direction in which Jake nodded.

At 3:15, they were riding across the bridge, headed for the open range.

The sky was moonless and black, but the smell of water and green things blew off the river.

As they jogged away from River Bend, Nike's head swung toward Ace.

Usually he was ridden by Pete, and Sam wondered if Nike, who couldn't see the rider on his back, was checking with Ace to make sure this new guy was okay.

"Don't see much," Jake said, eyes turned toward the Calico Mountains.

"Good," Sam said.

A dark red-orange stripe outlined the mountains. Sunrise was on its way.

They swung the horses left, toward Three Ponies and the shortcut to Aspen Creek.

Riding with Jake was different from riding with Jen. Instead of talking and laughing, Jake rode like a tracker.

Over the mountains, the red-orange stripe brightened into a serape of pinks.

Sam saw the silhouette of Jake's head lift to study the juniper and pinion branches that looked as if they'd been inked in black against that pink.

Seconds later, a covey of quail fretted and fluttered at the base of the pinions. Had he heard them or only sensed them? Knowing Jake, he might even have smelled them. He wouldn't miss the fresh scent of sagebrush creased by a bird's wing.

Sam tried to ride with the same focus. No matter how hard she listened, though, she didn't hear a hoof strike granite or the crunch of brush that meant mustangs were wending among the aspen trees to elude the riders.

If Hotspot was with the mustangs, would she stop, recognizing domestic horses as her own kind? It would be a lot handier if she'd come trotting up to them with Shy Boots by her side, Sam thought, yawning.

Nike slowed, then stopped.

"Brynna said Aspen Creek, but where'd you see that stud last?"

Sam didn't miss the challenge in Jake's voice. They were good friends, and she'd do almost anything for him. Almost. One thing she'd never do was reveal the Phantom's secret valley, and he knew it. Luckily, that wasn't the answer to his question.

"The last place I saw mustangs was by the box

canyon on the way up to Cowkiller Caldera," Sam said. "But that was a couple days ago."

"'Kay," Jake said, and instantly Nike's sorrel body lunged into a lope. The going between here and Aspen Creek was good, so Jake had decided to pick up the pace.

With a delighted snort, Ace matched Nike's speed and loped beside him.

Soon, the hills looked like lumpy dinosaurs' backs as the sun's gold corona brightened the sky.

They left the broad alkali flats behind. Underfoot, there was more grass, with only a few handprint-sized splashes of mineral white.

To Sam, the patches looked like snow sprouting sagebrush and tender grass.

The terrain plummeted downhill to Aspen Creek. Trees followed the water, but once a rider crossed the creek, the hillside rose again.

Wordless and careful, they rode downhill, then through a marshy area. The horses' hooves made sucking sounds and Ace pulled at the reins, asking for water.

While the horses drank, Sam turned to Jake.

"I know we don't have time today, but when do you want to go up to the box canyon? You know, to check the fence and look for prints and stuff."

"Let's see how today goes. Might be no reason to second-guess the sheriff."

He urged Nike, splashing, ahead, but Ace was still thirsty.

Jake was right, but Sam couldn't help feeling the sheriff had missed something important. Maybe she was just hoping he had.

Finally, her bay gelding raised his head and swung it around to nuzzle her boot with wet lips.

"Hey, wait for us," Sam said as Ace plodded after Nike.

Her yell disturbed the serenity around them, but the rustling didn't come from frightened birds.

What was it? Sam wondered. She stared hard between Jake's shoulder blades, waiting for him to turn toward the sound.

She was staring so hard at Jake's back, it took a few seconds for her to notice and interpret Ace's nicker.

He sensed mustangs. But where?

Sam's head swiveled from side to side.

She heard the crashing of a herd on the move and squinted through the half light up the gentle rise of a wooded hill. It sounded like the hooves were traveling in that direction.

Then, in a clearing, Sam saw two horses looking down on her.

Glowing like polished wood set against a curve of ivory, Hotspot stood beside the Phantom.

The stallion's ears pricked forward. His neck

turned left, then right. His shoulder bumped the mare aside. She backed up quickly before whirling in the direction of the rest of the herd.

"Jake," Sam hissed.

Jake had already seen the stallion, and so had Nike.

Gathering his reins and speaking softly, Jake reminded Nike to behave, but by then the Phantom was charging.

As the stallion thundered down the hill, the red gelding shied. Nike knew he must obey the Phantom, not the stranger on his back.

Chapter Fifteen ல

$\mathcal{S}$am heard a rushing sound, like a wave cresting. She saw the stallion's mane tossed back like wind-blown foam. He was a tidal wave of horse coming through the thicket of aspens, straight at Jake.

If he rammed Nike, the Phantom could take them all down in a tangle of horses and riders.

"No!" Sam yelled. "No, Z—"

In that moment of panic, she almost shouted the stallion's secret name. She bit it off, but maybe that hiss of sound made him swerve. Or maybe it had been a false charge, warning Nike and Jake away.

Ace's high-pitched whinny stabbed Sam's ears. Her wrists snapped as he tugged at the reins. Her cheek throbbed as Ace jounced his front hooves against the earth, struggling to follow the other mustangs.

Nike reared, and though Jake rode out the upheaval, he was working hard to quiet the horse. The Phantom was only yards away, his head bowed and neck full. His nostrils flared and his dark eyes flashed beneath torrents of forelock.

But he didn't cross the creek.

When Nike lowered to all four hooves, he trembled.

The stallion might have been invisible for all the attention Jake gave him. Jake concentrated on Nike, backing him and coaxing him, calming the horse with small tasks he could handle.

Sam watched the Phantom. His fierce stance, pawing at the earth until it flew in clumps from his hoof, was a warning. Even someone who'd never seen a fighting stallion would understand they'd cross the creek at their peril.

Satisfied by Nike's retreat, the Phantom pivoted and plunged after his fleeing herd.

Did he recognize me? Sam wondered. If he did, he didn't care.

"Ride back up the hill," Jake said. "If we can see his herd running, we might spot the Appaloosas."

Sam didn't waste time telling Jake she'd seen Hotspot. She hadn't seen Shy Boots.

Sam wheeled Ace, set her heels against his ribs, and rode. Nike joined in the pursuit, and when they reached the hilltop, both horses and riders were breathless.

"There," Sam said.

The Phantom's herd meandered across the plain below.

As always, the two blood bays showed first. Sam was able to pick out the big honey-colored lead mare and the pinto she'd named Pirate. Blacks, bays, and chestnuts moved at a steady walk, and she made out one Appaloosa. Only one.

"Where's Shy Boots?" Sam whispered, and when she looked at Jake, he shook his head.

Looking lost, Hotspot trailed the mustangs.

The lead mare didn't let her lag for long. With a squeal and snapping teeth, she forced the Appaloosa to join the rest of the herd.

Sam leaned forward until the saddle horn pressed into her stomach and her forearm rested against Ace's coarse black mane, as if moving just that much closer would show her what wasn't there.

Hotspot wouldn't have left without her colt if he'd been nearby.

Shy Boots was gone.

At the sudden sound of hooves, Sam spotted the white stallion galloping after his herd.

He seemed to skim above the earth, mane and tail lashing free around him. She could more easily believe he was flying than she could believe he was a killer.

Beside her, Jake tugged his black Stetson down.

"I want to go home," Sam said.

They'd ridden a long time in silence when a sage hen rose straight up in front of Ace. Feathers brushed his nose, and spooked him into a single, vigorous buck. After she settled the gelding, Sam's spirits picked up enough to ask Jake the question that had been plaguing her.

"There could be another explanation, right? The Phantom might not have killed Shy Boots."

"Sure," Jake said, but his sideways glance said that most of the other possibilities were no better.

So Sam made herself say the words. "A young foal alone won't live long on the range."

Hoofbeats filled in the silence for a minute, then Jake said, "If he's on the range."

"What do you mean?"

"Don't get your hopes up, but didn't you say the trailer had been messed with? And the fence taken down by hand?"

"That's what Sheriff Ballard said," Sam told him.

"It's a real long shot, Brat, but someone could've taken him."

Sam stared at Jake. She couldn't see Jake's eyes in the shade of his Stetson, and the skin over his high-carved cheekbones lay smooth.

He wasn't smiling or frowning as he said, "Just suppose someone was trying to steal them both—"

Sam's heart beat with crazy hope as she suggested, "Someone who didn't know horses."

"Especially if the stallion was nearby, Hotspot might have gotten away and she might not have noticed the foal wasn't right with her, until she was too far away to turn back."

"Or maybe she did turn back, but he'd stolen Shy Boots already."

Jake shrugged, without questioning the "he."

As they rode toward home, Sam felt something like relief. At least Hotspot was safe. Sam sighed and the muscles in her shoulders loosened.

Sam yawned. Three o'clock had been a long time ago.

When she and Jake arrived back at River Bend, Sam could hardly believe it was only lunchtime. But the ranch yard lay quiet, so Jen and the girls must be inside eating lunch.

"We found Hotspot," Sam said as they entered the kitchen.

"What?" Jen's voice cut over Jake's grumble.

"You found her!" Mikki celebrated by pumping a fist toward the rafters.

"I bet it was the skilled tracker who trailed her to where she was hiding," Gina said with a flirtatious grin.

Sam grabbed Jake's sleeve before he ducked out the kitchen door.

"You've got to eat," she told him, and Jake managed to fold himself into his place at the table without brushing anyone's elbow.

"Any sign of Shy Boots?" Jen asked.

"He wasn't with her," Sam said.

Silence seemed to press out from Sam until it filled the room. Dad had stayed silent, as if he'd known this would happen.

Cougar came slinking into the kitchen. In the quiet, Sam could hear the cat's tongue lap from his water dish.

"No sign of him anywhere?" Gram asked, and Sam realized she'd been drying her hands on a dish towel since they'd come into the kitchen. Everyone was shaken by the prospect of the foal being alone.

"Nothing," Jake confirmed.

"I'm still suspicious over that Karl Mannix," Gram said.

"Yeah, all this stuff happens and he takes off," Jen said.

"Yet Linc says they parted on friendly terms," Gram pointed out.

"I'm calling Ryan again," Sam said.

When all eyes turned to Gram, she dipped an arm toward the telephone. "Be my guest," she said.

"Ryan, this is Sam. We found Hotspot running with the Phantom's herd, but Karl Mannix is gone."

"Answer your stupid phone," Mikki yelled.

Sam hung up.

"I'd wonder if he'd even taken his cell phone with him, except that Linc said he talked with him," Jen said.

"No fair." Gina's whine made everyone stare. "Karl Mannix steals, like, thousands of dollars' worth of horses, and doesn't get caught. All I did was break a few windows and eat some candy, and the law's all over me."

Sam saw her own alarm reflected in Jen's eyes. Everything had been going well, but the HARP program wouldn't like the lesson Gina thought she'd learned.

"He's a man on the run," Jen pointed out.

"And we all hate him," Sam added.

When Gina didn't appear convinced, Sam looked to Mikki for help. The younger girl wore a faraway expression while her fingers plucked at her wispy blond hair. Suddenly, she grinned.

"And we're going to catch him. I know how to do it." Mikki bounced in her chair.

"How?" Jake asked.

He watched Mikki with such open respect that she blushed, straightened in her seat, and then, after shooting Gina a gloating glance, explained.

"Mr. Slocum said Mannix was a computer nerd. I think that *he* thinks, because you guys are all ranch people . . ." Mikki paused. "I don't mean that in a bad way, but you know, he probably figures you're not really—"

"Civilized?" Sam put in, recalling Mrs. Allen had made this suggestion, too.

"How about 'computer literate'?" Jen suggested.

"That's a better way to put it," Gina said, giggling.

"Yeah, he's the type who figures everyone's dumber than him, but I bet he's dumb enough to do this on the Internet, where anyone could catch him."

"That seems too easy," Jen said.

"Easy?" Gram chuckled. "Sounds to me like a wild-goose chase. I'm not sure I'd trust that sort of electronic gossip."

"I think Mikki's right about his attitude," Sam said. "Remember when Sheriff Ballard was giving Linc strategies for tracking down the horses? Mannix was astounded that a small-town sheriff knew so much."

"I love to see smug people get caught," Jen said with a sigh.

"I want to see him taken down," Mikki said.

It sounded too dramatic, like something Mikki had heard on television, but Sam could see she meant it.

"Remember that poor little colt," Mikki said.

"I couldn't forget if I wanted to," Sam said, and when she thought of her part in his disappearance, the marrow of her bones ached.

Mikki struck her fist against the table. She wanted more than justice. Mikki wanted revenge.

The gesture was like a bugle call. Gina, Jen, and Sam pushed back from the table, ready to get started.

"Two problems," Dad said. "First, Brynna's laptop, our only computer, is with her at Willow Springs. And second, you girls are supposed to be working with horses, not computers."

"This is about horses," Mikki insisted.

"I'm sure it would be okay," Gina added. "Please, Mr. Forster."

"Please." Mikki drew the word out in a high-pitched appeal.

Sam didn't blame the two girls, but they didn't know Dad. Begging made his resolve set up like concrete.

"We'll check with Brynna tonight," he said.

Mikki and Gina slumped and grumbled.

Sam met Jen's eyes, then Jake's. *Time to think fast, counselors.* Mikki and Gina were growing more disgruntled by the second.

What should they do?

"Mount up," Jake said.

"What?" Mikki asked.

"Get in the saddle. We'll play follow the leader."

"I've just been doing ground work," Gina said, looking to Jen for backup. "I haven't gotten on Popcorn yet."

"It's Tuesday. How long were you gonna wait?" Jake asked Jen.

"'Til tomorrow, like it says in the lesson plan."

Sam had seen sparks fly between her two best friends before, but this wasn't the time for it.

Before she could intercede, Jake realized it, too.

"Think she could start a half day early, if we keep it simple?" Jake asked.

Jen's expression grew hazy as she rewound a mental videotape of Gina's performance so far. Then, Jen nodded.

"She could, if we keep it simple."

"Gram, could Gina borrow Sweetheart?" Sam asked.

The aged pinto mare had once belonged to Sam's mother. When Mom died, Gram had taken Sweetheart as her own riding horse. Always responsive and well-mannered, the mare, at twenty-two years old, was safe as a rocking chair.

"Good idea, dear," Gram said. "She hasn't had a rider up for a while."

Gina swirled the bit of milk left in her glass around and around. Finally, she asked, "Does that mean she's going to be all spirited and stuff?"

"She'll be perfect," Sam promised.

Thirty minutes later, five riders explored the ranch. Sam took the lead on Ace, while Mikki rode Popcorn behind her. On Penny, Jen stayed just ahead of Gina and Sweetheart, while Jake rode Nike at the rear, watching for problems.

At a flat-footed walk, Ace led them out to the bridge, but didn't cross it. He came back past the ranch house and circled the barn pasture. Dark Sunshine watched the procession and Tempest nickered that she wanted to come along.

When Sam reined Ace aside and let Mikki take the lead, Popcorn's hooves stuttered. He felt his rider's lack of confidence, but his uncertainty didn't last. A minute later, the albino gelding stepped out at a brisk walk and the others followed.

Mikki let Jen take over, but she took her turn for only a few minutes. Then Gina became the leader.

"Doin' fine," Jake said, two or three minutes into Gina's turn.

But Sweetheart was picking up speed, ambling toward the barn.

"What should I do?" Gina said,

"Move your hand to the right," Jake said. "Good."

Sweetheart obeyed instantly. Gina wrinkled her nose in delight and turned to Jake.

"My hero," she said.

Jake shrugged. "You told her it's not quittin' time."

He might not know it, Sam thought, but Jake had saved the afternoon from becoming a pouting competition between Gina and Mikki.

Although he was only helping out as a HARP counselor for the money, he was good at it.

When Brynna arrived home, she agreed to Mikki's plan to stalk Karl Mannix on the Internet. As soon as the dinner dishes were washed, the girls got started.

Sam and Gina quickly discovered their fingers didn't fly as quickly as Mikki's and Jen's, so they made lists of ideas.

"Just in case, we should check lost-and-found sites—"

"Places you can post horses for sale—"

"And brand inspectors—"

Sam's pencil jotted down each item, and then she realized Gina was shaking her index finger at an invisible idea.

"We'll post a reward leading to the, um, you know, to the—"

"Recovery," Jen suggested as her fingers went on dancing over the keyboard.

"Right!" Gina said. "We describe Shy Boots and say there's a reward for his recovery. That way, if Mannix still has the colt, and he responds, the sheriff can arrest him!"

"Yeah!" Mikki said. "And we'll use my e-mail address, because he couldn't possibly know it."

Mikki and Gina wiggled like puppies, delighted with their deceit.

"We are so sneaky," Mikki said.

"But in a good way," Gina shouted to Brynna as she peeked in from the kitchen.

And Sam decided that was progress, of a kind.

Chapter Sixteen ❧

Sam and Blaze sat on the bridge over the La Charla River. With her cheek pressed against one wooden rail of the bridge, Sam looked down at ripples turned silver by the moon.

She'd been awake for nineteen hours, and though she was definitely tired, she was just as definitely not sleepy. The Phantom wouldn't come to the river tonight, and she was almost glad.

Glad might be the wrong word, Sam thought, but she felt relieved.

The Phantom had not been friendly to her today. He certainly hadn't come to her like—what was it Dad had said?—a lapdog.

In fact, the Phantom hadn't indicated by even a

flick of his ear that he'd recognized her.

So she didn't have to feel guilty about him tonight. And though Hotspot must miss her foal, she'd soon find her place in the herd. She'd probably be a part of it until autumn.

Brynna had insisted there was no way BLM would finance a special gather to capture a tame horse gone astray.

We can't be running mustangs with a helicopter just because Linc Slocum wants us to, Brynna had said. *In fact, if it turns out the horse was freed intentionally to run with the wild ones, Linc may have some penalties to pay.*

Sam sighed, and Blaze, dozing next to her, opened his eyes to give her hand a lick.

The silver ripples seemed to melt and coat the entire river. Sam blinked, trying to stay awake.

Shy Boots was still lost. More than anything Sam wanted to find him. She had to think. She had to make a plan. But maybe she'd close her eyes for just a minute.

In Sam's dream, she rode the Phantom in a game they'd never played before. Three silk scarves were hidden in the desert and she had to find them.

Riding the stallion bareback, she galloped over bone-white alkali flats, hand shading her eyes against a golden glare.

An emerald-green scarf fluttered from a sagebrush. Holding a handful of the Phantom's mane in one hand, Sam leaned over to snag the scarf with her fingers.

Pink and orange like the dawn sky, the second scarf blew on the wind. Sam only had to sit straight astride the stallion for the strip of silk to twine around her brow and remain there, blowing behind as if she, too, had a mane.

The Phantom's slender legs raced miles across the desert, slanting as she searched north and south, east and west; but the last scarf could not be found.

A mirage of yellow shimmered on the horizon. As she and the Phantom drew closer, a figure waved from inside it.

"He knows where it is," she told the Phantom, but the stallion swerved, refusing to go closer, and Sam was falling . . .

Her cheek hit the wooden deck of the bridge, and she woke up.

"Ow!" she said, mostly to Blaze. "Of course it couldn't be the cheek that was already hurt," she said, rubbing her face.

The Border collie panted and cocked his head to one side, looking a little worried.

"I'm okay," she said, rising stiffly to her knees, and then to her bare feet. "And I think I'm finally ready for bed."

The HARP girls' riding lessons progressed faster than expected. By Thursday, Gina could catch Popcorn, groom him, tack him up, and ride him around the round pen alone. Mikki rode Popcorn at a walk, jog, and lope, and Dark Sunshine had eaten a sugar cube from her hand.

But the hunt for the horse thief had fizzled, and Ryan still hadn't returned Sam's calls.

With only two days left of the HARP session, the summer heat closed around them like a fist.

The next day was the Fourth of July, but with no clues about Shy Boots's or Karl Mannix's whereabouts, and no breezes to cool them, it was hard to look forward to a day spent in the relentless sun.

At midmorning, Gina and Mikki were playing follow-the-leader again when lightning crackled across the sky, then rain pelted down.

For an hour, they tried riding in yellow slickers, but Penny bucked at the strange sound, and Popcorn balked. No matter how Gina urged him on, the albino hung his head and let raindrops drip from his white nose.

As they stripped the tack from the horses and turned them out, Jake didn't quit. He swung into Witch's saddle.

"What's he doing?" Jen asked, using wet fingers to polish the fog from her glasses.

Sam stared at Jake. Dressed in a dark slicker and Stetson, Jake ignored the downpour. He jogged Witch through a figure eight, slid her to a stop, then asked her to reverse the pattern.

"Sometimes even I can't figure him out," Sam said, but she was remembering Jake's accident last autumn.

The horse who'd slipped in the mud and crushed Jake's leg had been young, but the accident could have happened to any horse. She'd bet Jake was giving Witch a little extra schooling. The next time he had to gallop her in the mud, Witch would be ready.

Sam realized she was watching a major difference between Ryan and Jake. Ryan tried to buy his way out of trouble, but Jake prepared to stand up against it.

"Tell me about the *desert*, again?" Gina asked Sam, as they carried the saddles back to the tack room.

"I already said it wasn't like the Sahara," Sam grumbled. "But this doesn't usually happen until August."

"I guess we can work on the computer some more," Mikki said. "Brynna left it home again."

"Not me," Gina said, looking back toward the middle of the ranch yard. "I'm staying outside."

"What for?" Mikki asked. Looking down at her boots, she tried to avoid quickly filling puddles. "Are you going swimming?"

But Sam followed Gina's gaze to Jake.

"Jake brought a baseball," Gina said offhandedly. "He said he'd throw it around with me."

"In this?" Mikki said. "You're crazy."

"I was starting pitcher for my team before I quit, and I was never rained out." Sniffing and shrugging, she added, "Maybe the coach will take me back."

Sam bit back the encouragement she wanted to offer. It might have the opposite effect, and Gina was doing fine on her own.

The kitchen was warm. When she saw Blaze lying on the floor in front of the stove, Sam tried to remember her dream.

"Can't get him to go outside, and he's not easy to work around," Gram said, shaking her head.

Sam stared at Blaze, and suddenly she remembered the very end of her dream. Something yellow had come toward her and the answer to some question was inside.

"I hope you girls have worked up an appetite. The power's been flickering," Gram said, looking up at the kitchen lights overhead, "so I'm going to make an early lunch."

The fireplace roared with golden flames. Sam warmed herself in front of it, staring toward Brynna's laptop, which sat alone, left on a chair beyond the fire's warmth.

"Want to go first?" Sam asked Jen, nodding at the computer.

"No, it's not even charged up. You'll have to plug it in over there." Jen motioned toward the far chair.

"I've had it with the Internet," Jen said, as she and Mikki set up a board game on the living room's big coffee table.

"Maybe he's laying low for a little while," Mikki said. "That's what a smart thief would do."

"Oxymoron," Jen muttered.

"Who's a moron?" Mikki snapped.

"No, 'smart thief' is an oxymoron," Jen explained

as she searched in the game box for directions. "An oxymoron is a seeming contradiction"—Mikki shot Sam a despairing glance as Jen went on—"like, you can't be smart and be a thief, because thieves go to jail, and who—"

"Let's just play the game," Mikki said.

After polishing the rain streaks from her glasses, Jen agreed.

Sam crawled on the rug to plug in the little computer, then sat in the corner chair, shivering at first, then getting more and more absorbed in her search.

Once, she glanced out the window, hoping Hotspot and Shy Boots were both someplace safe and warm. Then she returned to her research with stronger determination.

She heard Gram call out the kitchen door for Jake and Gina to come in for lunch. She heard Mikki's delight over the menu of grilled-cheese sandwiches and tomato soup, but everything seemed to be far away. Sam kept pecking at the keyboard until Gina burst into the living room.

"I've got it!" Gina shouted.

Blaze barked and frolicked around Gina as she shed her wet slicker and motioned for Sam to give over the laptop.

"I thought of something we haven't tried."

Sam stood beside Gina as she attacked the little laptop.

"Blaze, I like you, too, but get away," Gina said,

elbowing the Border collie's inquiring muzzle.

"I think he likes you because you smell like a wet dog," Sam joked.

"Ha ha," Gina said absently. "There. Remember on preview night at the carnival, how that lady said she only bought animals from *reputable* dealers? Well that must mean there are bad ones, right?"

As Gina's fingers tapped away, Sam remembered thinking the same thing herself.

"So, we're gonna search . . ." Gina's voice trailed off. "There's Patty's Pronto Petting Zoo. That's the lady we talked to, right? Wanna look? Oh, she posts next-day pictures from events she takes the animals to. . . ."

Sam sighed. For a minute, she'd hoped Gina really did have a great idea. Something obvious they'd missed. Now, she gazed at the website's photos, disheartened.

"Yeah, well, I don't think pictures of goats at Jamie Smith's fifth birthday party are really—wait! Gina, go back!"

Chills cascaded down Sam's arms. Had she really seen what she thought she had?

"Yeah, you're liking that site now that you saw some horses," Gina joked, "but Patty's okay. I'll search for—"

"No! You have to go back!" Sam said. "In the background, I think I saw—I'm sure I saw Shy Boots."

Gina looked up, staring at Sam with rounded eyes.

"Hurry," Sam whispered.

Gina looked down, shaking her head.

"Probably it wasn't him," she murmured. "Patty seemed so nice."

"There." Sam knelt beside Gina as the computer image materialized with infuriating slowness.

"Are you sure?" Gina asked. "It's kind of hard to see."

"Jen! Gram!" Sam shouted to be heard above the thunderclap. "Come in here, quick!"

"We're losing it!" Gina moaned.

The living room went black, except for the crackling fireplace.

"Mercy, Samantha," Gram said as the kitchen door swung open. "It's just a power failure, nothing to scream about."

Against her best judgment, Sheriff Ballard's secretary patched Gram through to the sheriff at the fairgrounds.

"I certainly hope you saw what you think you did," Gram said, covering the mouthpiece while she waited.

"We did, Gram. Right?" Sam looked at the other girls. They all hesitated except Gina, who gave a slight nod. "Well, I saw him. Cross my heart," Sam crisscrossed a finger over her chest to underscore her certainty.

"Hello?" Gram said into the phone. "Heck, this is Grace Forster, and I know how busy you are. Pickpockets? In Darton County?" Gram shook her head. "I can hardly credit that, but I sure wouldn't want your job. At any rate, it's about that Appaloosa colt."

Sam watched Gram's eyebrows climb her forehead.

"Yes, it's just that—" Gram broke off, listening.

"Try, Gram!" Sam urged her.

Rolling her eyes like a teenager, Gram plunged into the conversation one more time.

"Of course, Heck, but it seems the colt will be there at the fairgrounds tomorrow at the petting zoo."

Sam realized she and the other three girls were crowded shoulder to shoulder. In the flickering glow from the candle Gram had lit after the power failure, with their rain-bedraggled hair, they looked a little like witches.

Finally, Gram sighed.

"I understand. Of course. You have your hands full with people who want your help. Thanks again, Sheriff." Gram nodded and glanced up at Sam. "I'll tell her. We'll probably see you tomorrow."

"What?" Sam asked as Gram hung up the phone and went to the stove, where the grilled-cheese sandwiches she'd made before the power failure were waiting.

"It's really quite simple," Gram said. She put the sandwiches and bowls of cooling tomato soup on the table. "Linc refuses to file a police report."

"So, it's like a crime wasn't committed, even though somebody sold that colt to the petting zoo," Jen said.

"That's about the size of it," Gram said. "Now eat your lunch before it's stone cold. You can think at the same time."

During lunch, Sam decided to give Ryan Slocum one last chance.

"You're wasting your breath," Gina said.

"You don't know that," Mikki snapped.

"I think he's in on it with his dad," Gina said.

Sam was about to ask Jen what she thought of calling Ryan, but then she realized it didn't matter. She was going to call Ryan no matter what anyone said.

She drew a deep breath and punched in the telephone number.

Sam almost dropped the phone when Ryan answered.

Beside Sam, Jen looked startled, too.

"What is it?" Jen asked. "You're holding the telephone as if it just turned into a snake."

"Ryan?" Sam asked.

"Who else would be answering my cell phone?" Ryan retorted.

"Ryan, this is Samantha. We've found your colt, but—"

"Shy Boots is supposed to be on his way to England. Where did you find him?"

"Why would he be on his way to England?" Sam asked.

"Because I'm going home."

"You're going back to England?" Sam repeated, ducking away from Jen, who tried to grab the phone away. "Why?"

"If you will stop asking questions and answer a few—"

Ryan's arrogance worked like a match to the fuse of a firecracker.

"Don't even try to boss me around, Ryan. It worked last time, but never again. I should have listened to my own good sense. Not only did you use me, you lied to me."

Sam glimpsed Jen's amazement. Her eyes were wide and her mouth agape. Gram, Mikki, and Gina looked pretty much the same.

In the silence, Sam wondered if Ryan had hung up.

She listened so hard, she thought she heard blood swishing through the veins in her ear.

Finally, Ryan spoke. "Everything I told you was true, except for coming back that night. It's not like the horses were stranded there. I wrote Karl Mannix a check to pay their fare to England."

"But he didn't do what you wanted him to. Someone—probably Mannix—ripped down the fence. Hotspot is running with the mustangs. And Shy Boots is in a petting zoo."

"I made an excellent plan," Ryan said stubbornly.

"Which did not work," Sam said, spacing the words out so that he couldn't miss a single one.

"I paid him a sufficient amount—"

"So what? Sometimes you have to do things yourself," Sam insisted.

She might have been giving herself a pep talk, and it was a good thing. The other four faces stared at her as if she were crazy.

"I would have been waiting for them in England," Ryan said in a pouty tone.

"Why, Ryan?"

"Isn't it painfully clear?" he asked. "I don't fit in, in Nevada."

Sam remembered Ryan saying he was the last person who could teach Shy Boots to be a Western horse. She also remembered what Sheriff Ballard had said about him.

"Give it time," she told him. "You've only been here a few months. I was *born* in the West, and I'm still figuring things out."

"That's very kind of you, but—"

"No, Ryan, I'm not being kind. I'm telling you to cowboy up."

Jen flung her arms out like wings, then mouthed the words, *What are you doing?*

Sam closed her eyes. She had to do this her way.

"Who do you think you are —?" Ryan barked.

"Act insulted if you like, but it won't help. Your father refuses to file a police report. That means the sheriff can't do anything. If you want Shy Boots back, he'll be at the Fourth of July carnival, at the fairgrounds, in Patty's Petting Zoo."

Sam hung up. Her hand was still trembling on the phone, when she realized she was out of breath.

"Good going, Sam," Jen said. "You said what needed to be said. I just hope he heard it."

"I hope that really was Shy Boots on the website," Mikki giggled.

With an admiring smile, Gina took off her baseball cap and hung it on Sam's head backwards.

The Fourth of July dawned sunny.

"It's like it never rained a drop," Mikki said as she finished drying the last breakfast dish.

Gina snatched the plate from Mikki and stuck it in the cupboard. Jen straightened the tablecloth with an impatient twitch and Sam shouted up the stairs.

"Brynna, are you ready?"

Dad called down something Sam couldn't understand, but his tone said she knew better than to shout.

"Honey, what's your rush?" Gram asked. "The parade won't begin for another hour."

"We might not be able to find a parking place," Sam said, though she and Gram both knew she wanted to get there and look for Shy Boots.

"You girls got up so early," Gram said.

In fact, they'd hardly slept. They'd chattered through a dozen what-if plans for bringing the colt back home.

Their first choice was to have Sheriff Ballard impound the colt. If that didn't work, they'd talk to Patty and try to make her understand what had happened. If all else failed, they planned to steal Shy Boots back.

"Aren't you warm, dear?" Gram asked, considering Sam's sweatshirt.

"I want to be prepared in case it rains," Sam said.

"It'll soak up water like a sponge," Dad commented as he came into the kitchen.

Sam gave a nervous laugh. Underneath her sweatshirt, she wore one of Brynna's uniform shirts.

It was Gina who'd remembered that Patty wore a khaki shirt just like the ones Brynna wore with her uniform.

"Wear it," Gina told Sam. "If anyone notices you carrying Shy Boots away, they'll think you work for Patty."

"Have you ever tried to carry a horse?" Jen had asked, but she'd agreed to go along.

Sam was still more worried about being a bad influence on Gina than she was about moving the colt, but she couldn't come up with a better scheme to reclaim Shy Boots.

"There's been a slight change of plans," Dad said,

looking over the girls' heads at Gram. "If you all can get along without us, I think we'll be staying home. Brynna just can't seem to shake off this flu."

"That's a shame," Gram said, "but we'll be fine, won't we, girls?"

They agreed in a chorus, but as they walked out of the house, toward the Buick, Gram held Sam back a moment.

"Dear, I almost forgot to give you the message Sheriff Ballard asked me to pass along to you yesterday."

"What's that?" Sam asked dubiously.

"He said you wouldn't like juvenile hall."

Chapter Seventeen ❧

𝒫arade horses' hooves clattered on asphalt.

Vendors sold cotton candy, caramel apples, and popcorn from trays suspended around their necks.

Excited children clung to balloons and tugged their parents along the sidewalk outside the fairground gates to the carnival inside.

"You can do this," Gina assured Sam as they hurried toward the blue-and-white-striped awning that shaded the petting zoo. "It's the right thing to do."

"If he's here, I'm going to the sheriff," Sam insisted.

Doing the wrong thing for the right reason was a bad idea. She'd learned the hard way.

Sheriff Ballard appeared just a few feet away. He

walked through the crowd, adjusting a knob on his walkie-talkie.

"There he is," Jen said.

Sam felt stronger with the sheriff nearby. Even though he'd told Gram that he couldn't arrest anyone without a complaint, she'd bet he'd back her up if Shy Boots were here.

"If only Ryan were here, too," Sam said with a sigh.

She hadn't really expected him to show up. Ryan let other people smooth out his life's complications.

Just the same, Shy Boots deserved help, even if Ryan Slocum didn't.

"Let's go see if the colt's here," Sam said. "Before Sheriff Ballard gets busy with something else. Gram—"

"Samantha, you go ahead. I'll stand right here and watch the parade. I trust you not to do something silly."

For a second Sam thought she heard thunder.

Was it an omen? Or would this rescue be rained out?

"Drums," Gina said, and a giddy smile lit her face. "The bands are coming. It's showtime!"

Last night Gina had made a big deal of using noise to cover Shy Boots's rescue.

Sam met Jen's eyes. Together, they shrugged. Just when it looked like Gina had turned the corner toward being a *reformed* burglar, she got excited over the prospect of breaking the law.

Wending their way through the crowd, all four girls jogged to the fence surrounding the petting zoo.

"Goats, chickens, rabbits, more goats . . . ," Gina muttered as they stared inside. "No colt, and no Patty."

Over the heads of children in line, Sam scanned the petting zoo.

Gina was wrong.

Shy Boots lay in a corner, alone, with his gangly chocolate-brown legs folded.

Sam's pulse pounded louder than the kettle drums in the parade. Shy Boots was here. He was safe. And Hotspot was running free with a well-guarded herd.

Neither horse she'd put in danger had been hurt. Sam exhaled and felt suddenly lighter. She'd been so lucky.

"Go get the sheriff," Sam said, turning to Mikki.

"I'll stay with the baby," Mikki crooned with a sugary voice. "You go get the sheriff."

"Come on," Jen said, and towing Mikki along by the wrist, she disappeared into the crowd.

"Do you see Patty?" Gina hissed.

Sam shook her head.

A college-aged guy in a khaki shirt stood at the gate, selling tickets and shooing kids into the petting zoo.

Another lie, Sam thought. Patty had claimed that where her animals were, she was, but she was nowhere in sight.

"Careful," called the guy at the gate. "Don't let the gate shut on that pig. And hey, ducks shouldn't eat licorice. Knock it off."

How could she make this work? Sam wondered.

Could she ask this guy, who wasn't the boss, if he'd bought Shy Boots from a nerdy-looking man who sniffed a lot and had watery eyes? She could, but he probably wouldn't know. And he certainly wouldn't hand Shy Boots over when Sam explained the foal had been stolen.

When the guy glanced up, clearly bored, Sam tried to look sympathetic. He responded right away.

"Sheesh, my mom is a nutcase," he muttered, then as he realized no other children stood in line, he glanced toward the pitching booth, instead of watching the children in the petting pen.

Had Jen and Mikki found the sheriff yet?

"This couldn't be better," Gina whispered. "That guy isn't paying attention. You could walk right in there and take the colt."

"I won't do that!"

"I'm just saying." Gina sighed.

"And I'm just going in with him," Sam said.

"I'll create a distraction," Gina said.

"I don't need a distraction," Sam told her. "I'm just watching him until the sheriff gets here."

Sam edged closer to the open gate as three children ran out of the petting zoo.

Shy Boots's ears turned toward Sam as if he'd

recognized her, but it wasn't possible.

Maybe, Sam thought, catching the gate with the edge of her tennis shoe, he recognized escape.

By the time she looked up again, Gina had strolled over to the pitching booth.

At the same time Sam realized she didn't have an admission ticket, the guy in the khaki shirt called out to her.

"Which one's with you?" he asked.

It only took Sam a second to understand he thought she was baby-sitting one of the four kids left inside the pen.

Sam pointed vaguely. The guy nodded that she could go in, then turned back as a landslide of tin milk bottles drew his attention back to the pitching booth.

"Wow, look at her throw!" the guy in the khaki shirt yelled to no one in particular.

Ponytail tucked through the back of her baseball cap, Gina had knocked down all the milk bottles and earned another turn.

When she turned back and gave the petting zoo guy a dazzling smile, Sam could see it was genuine. Gina had found something besides burglary that made her happy.

But where was the sheriff?

Sam pulled off her sweatshirt and knotted it around her waist. She only did it because the morning was heating up.

She had no need for a disguise.

"Shy Boots," she whispered.

Brown velvet ears swiveled to catch her voice and the colt's throat trembled in a silent nicker.

"Here, sweet baby."

Gravel pricked Sam's knees through her jeans as she knelt beside the colt.

Unsure of her intentions, Shy Boots scrabbled up on all four hooves.

Sam touched the belt on her jeans. If she slipped it loose, she could drape it around the colt's neck and lead him right out of here.

He leads? she'd asked Ryan, that day in the box canyon.

Quite nicely, Ryan had bragged, and he'd been right.

It was tempting, but she would not do it, even though Boots looked down at her, blinked his long-lashed eyes, and stepped forward.

"Samantha."

It wasn't a voice she'd expected to hear.

It wasn't Jen's voice or Mikki's or Sheriff Ballard's. Behind her, Sam heard the smooth British voice of Ryan Slocum.

Resting a hand on the colt's neck, Sam turned just as the gate to the petting zoo squeaked open and Ryan came in.

He was dressed for a fancy dance. Or at least a nice restaurant. He wore a long-sleeved white shirt with the cuffs turned up and something silver stuck through to hold them in place. Mirror-polished shoes shone below black slacks, and Sam would bet everything she owned, except Ace, that the white limousine idling in the parking lot had brought Ryan from the airport.

"What are you doing here?" Sam asked.

"I came to fill out the paperwork my father won't, so that I can take back my horse," he said.

"In that limousine?" Sam joked, but Ryan was slipping his own leather belt free of loops and getting ready to put it around the colt's neck.

"If necessary," he said.

But Ryan's proud attitude changed when Shy Boots recognized him. Suddenly, the colt's ears came alert. His nostrils whuffled open and closed, and his tiny brush of a tail whisked from side to side.

"Hello, boy," Ryan greeted him.

"Hey, what do you think you're doing?" the khaki-shirted guy shouted when he saw Ryan's makeshift halter.

"Taking my horse," Ryan answered.

"Uh, Ryan, aren't you skipping a few steps?"

Ryan's raised eyebrow challenged Sam and the petting zoo attendant.

"Like filling out the police report," Sam said in a leading voice.

"Ah, yes," Ryan said.

The attendant was already rushing their way.

Before he got inside, though, Sam saw Jen and Mikki with Sheriff Ballard.

"You're not going anywhere," the guy yelled, though neither Sam nor Ryan had tried to leave. "Here comes the sheriff. They're trying to take my horse!" he shouted.

"Ownership of that particular horse might be in dispute," Sheriff Ballard said patiently.

Sam listened to the conversation between Patty's son and Sheriff Ballard, but she also watched Jen.

Her friend had had a crush on Ryan for several months, and sometimes he seemed to return it. But Sam saw the strain between them now. Jen stayed outside the petting zoo pen, and Ryan stayed inside with Shy Boots.

The sheriff was taking a statement from Patty's son, and though Sam still made no move to leave, Sheriff Ballard raised his eyes from his notebook, pointed at Sam, and said, "Wait."

After that juvenile hall message the sheriff had asked Gram to convey, Sam thought hard about what she'd done. As far as she could tell, she was in the clear.

". . . mom should have been here by now," Patty's son was saying. "I don't know what the deal is, but she didn't steal the horse. I was home when this guy came by—middle-aged, nerdy—and he sold her the orphan."

He had to be talking about Karl Mannix, but

where was Mannix now? Sam wondered.

"Did you happen to overhear his name?" Sheriff Ballard asked.

"No, but my mom will have it. She got a bill of sale. She's real particular about things like that."

"Did he explain how he came to have the colt?"

The guy shrugged. "Are you trying to say it's, like, stolen? Because all I heard was that the mother horse died, and my mom was actually okay with buying the colt because she has this donkey who had a colt or whatever, and the donkey just adopted him."

Shy Boots began nibbling Sam's shirt, then making sucking noises.

"He's hungry," Ryan said to the guy. "Do you have a bottle?"

"No, I don't have a bottle," he said, sounding a little offended. "My mom was supposed to have brought the donkey twenty minutes ago. Hey, I gotta go sell tickets," he said, noticing the line forming by the petting zoo. "And my mother will kill me if kids are in there unsupervised."

Sheriff Ballard closed his notebook and looked at Sam.

"I can explain everything," she said.

Raising one hand to cover her face in embarrassment, even though she didn't know why, Sam grazed her cut cheek. It hurt.

"Sheriff," Ryan said before the sheriff could question Sam, "I'll be glad to file the report my father hasn't. Clearly you know the colt's been stolen, and I daresay you have a guess who's to blame."

"Better than that," Sheriff Ballard's smile showed from beneath his sandy mustache. "I have casts of tire tracks and Vibram-soled shoes."

"Wow," Gina said in admiration.

"I got 'em before it rained," the sheriff said. "I just couldn't help myself."

Karl Mannix would be caught then, Sam thought. That would be great.

While the sheriff stepped aside to call in Ryan's charges, a rickety horse trailer came through the fairgrounds gates.

All at once, Shy Boots lunged and neighed. Ryan needed both hands on the belt to keep the colt from pulling free.

"I believe his lunch is coming," Ryan said, and if he was uncomfortable because a braying burro was nursemaid to his colt, Ryan didn't show it.

"So I researched the term, 'cowboy up,'" Ryan said to Sam.

"Yeah?" Sam saw the other girls move closer to the petting-zoo fence. Now that she wasn't angry anymore, the way she'd scolded Ryan was a little embarrassing.

"My understanding," Ryan went on, "is that it means I'm to catch my own horse, saddle my own horse and, if a time should come when he's beyond help and suffering, shoot my own horse."

"I guess so," Sam said.

"Everything I read could be a description of Jake Ely and your father," he added, nodding at Sam. "And yours." He nodded at Jen.

In the gap of silence, Sam noticed Ryan had left out his own father.

"And since you have better bloodlines for this than I, perhaps you can just school me like a yearling. That's about how long I'll give the process," Ryan said. "Otherwise, I'm bound for England again, and Boots can see how he likes the smell of fog and heather instead of sage and sun."

Sam smoothed her hands down Shy Boots's back. He hadn't been neglected while he was here, but his fidgeting said he recognized the burro's voice.

"One last thing before Boots goes to his foster mother," Ryan said. "Can I convince you to take me out on the range and introduce me to the stallion who's stolen Hotspot?"

"Never," Jen called into him.

"She's right," Sam said, smiling. "I won't take you to visit the Phantom. It's not safe for him to get too accustomed to people. So I guess you'll just have to live with that."

Ryan accepted the teasing with a shrug and probably had no idea he'd already picked up a cowboy gesture. He sure didn't know why she was laughing.

"Well then," Ryan said. "If you won't guide me out there, you might be surprised. It shouldn't take long for me to find my own way."

Should she take Ryan's words as a threat or a promise?

Sam didn't know, but as memory showed her the gleaming Appaloosa mare standing beside the wild white stallion, she knew the pair was up to the challenge.

From
Phantom Stallion
❧ 16 ❧
THE WILDEST HEART

"You need to leave the ranch," Jake said. "They never should have put the propane tank so close to the house."

Sam hadn't noticed the tank of propane Mrs. Allen used as heating fuel. Now, she did. The white tank looked like a small submarine, but it was filled with flammable gas. If the tank got too hot, it would explode.

"I'm outta here," Callie said, though she didn't take a step. "I trust Queen to take care of herself."

Jake looked satisfied as he motioned for the girls to walk ahead of him.

Callie watched Sam.

Sam set her teeth against each other. How could she balance her safety with that of the horses?

This was no time to bicker with Jake, but she said, "The lady at the fire department told me to wait for your dad, since he's the chief."

Jake's eyes widened. Sam could see he was offended, but just for a second.

"C'mon," he said, then strode toward the green fire truck parked outside the ranch gates.

Sam followed, but she only glanced at Luke Ely and the other guys in yellow turnouts clustered around him. They were all staring at the fire, and Sam stopped stonestill as her eyes followed theirs.

The fire had quadrupled in size. It had burned just a few yards along the fence line before veering away from the sanctuary pasture. Now it gobbled cheatgrass, leaving a black scorch behind as it swooped toward the foothills.

"Stop it!" Sam shouted, then she turned to Jake. "Can't you please stop the fire?"

For an instant, Jake's eyes showed he was her friend, the guy she'd grown up with.

"It's okay, Brat," he said, in a soothing tone. "It's burnin' away from us."

"I know," she said. "I'm not scared, it's . . ."

Jake's sympathy got all mixed up with her mental images of wild things fleeing hungry flames.

"The animals," Sam said, but while she tried to focus her thoughts, Jake returned to the firefighter's attitude he'd pulled on along with his turnouts.

"Our first responsibility is to protect people and structures," he said.

"But the people and structures are just fine!" Sam cried.

Frustration kept swelling inside Sam. Either Jake and the other firefighters were blind, or she was missing something. That had to be it, because they couldn't all be so hard-hearted. Could they?

As if he'd heard, Jake's brother Quinn surrendered his position on the hose to another man.

Skinny and tall, Quinn had porcupine-sharp crew-cut hair. He looked nothing like Jake as he strode toward them, carrying his helmet by the chin strap. Quinn was on student council at school and he'd helped her pull a trick or two on Jake, but once he reached them, his voice was honey-sweet, as if he were trying to calm her, too.

"Don't worry, you're safe," Quinn said.

"Who cares about *my* safety?" she began.

"You're always safe in the black," Quinn went on, as he pointed. "The first flames burned along the fence line. So even if the wind shifts and the fire comes back this way, you're okay. There's nothing for it to burn in the black."

When Sam waved her hands, he stopped talking, eyebrows raised in surprise. "I'm not worried about getting hurt. The fire is going up the canyon."

Quinn shot a quick glance at his brother, but Jake's expression reminded Sam of a closed door.

"It might burn that far, depending on the winds," Quinn said, squinting toward the hills. "Luckily, there's only cheatgrass between here and there. Really, it's doin' a good job of clearing things out. Lots of ranchers apply for permits and do a controlled burn so that they can plant. Mrs. Allen doesn't have to go to all that trouble."

All at once, Jake and Quinn stiffened, shrugged,

and went back to work as their dad approached.

Luke Ely was taller than Dad. His pronounced cheekbones and long jaw made him look like a man who was used to giving orders and having them obeyed. Sam knew Jake's dad had a great smile, but it was hard to picture it. As he came her way, he looked every inch a fire chief.

"It'd be a good idea to get those older horses out of here," he said to Callie. "They suffer from smoke inhalation just like people."

"Got it," Callie said, and her car keys were already in her hand as she left.

"Now, what's up with you?" he asked Sam.

Jake's dad sounded impatient, but faintly amused. Maybe.

"Quinn and Jake were both telling me there's no reason to fight the fire over there," Sam said, pointing. "And, I understand about you having to stay here and protect homes and barns first, but since it's all burned off—"

"It isn't," Luke interrupted. "It's burnin' spotty, because of moisture in the low places."

Sam swallowed hard as he indicated the place where she'd left the paint cans. She couldn't see them from here, but she could imagine dampness from the passing storm. It probably wouldn't be damp enough, Sam thought, as she heard more crackling.

"There's plenty left to burn if it turns back this way," Luke said. "That's why I left Nate down there with what equipment I could spare, and that's why we're taking a stand here."

The sound of a distressed neigh made Sam turn away from Luke. She squinted back toward the ranch yard. She could make out Callie in the corral and see Ace trotting uneasily around it. She could see only one pinto. Callie must have already loaded the other, but now she was battling Judge. Tossing his black mane, the old gelding reared, huffed, and resisted the pull on the halter rope.

"Samantha." Luke's voice jerked her attention back. "I need you to return to the house and stay there, if you're not leaving with Callie."

"I'm not," she said.

Callie drove past, windows rolled up against the smoke, but Sam could see she was frowning.

Sam didn't wave. She drew a breath, trying to ask more, explain more, but her eyes were fixed on a tower of smoke mingling with the gray clouds. She couldn't tell them apart. Smoke veiled the sun, turning it into a tan disk surrounded by a dull yellow ring. Everywhere the smoke wavered.

Fire didn't have a mind of its own. If it did, she'd think the flames were trying to decide which direction to charge next.

"Sam, you're going to have to spit it out," Luke snapped. "I've got duties, here."

Sam's fists curled so tightly, her fingernails bit into her palms.

"If the fire keeps burning toward the hills, it'll get into the canyons. My dad says they'll act just like a chimney."

Luke gave a nod, but then a tone from his radio distracted him. After a short sentence, he turned back to her.

"Wyatt's right. That area's a disaster waiting to happen. It hasn't burned off in years, which means there's lots of fuel.

"It looks awful when you see black, charred trees where a fire's gone through, but a fire can be a blessing. Old brush is gone. Big animals can move through areas that have been too dense for them. New seeds get sun for the first time and the ashes act like fertilizer. That's how nature does it and we've been interferin', settin' ourselves up—"

As Luke turned to his radio again, Sam rubbed her arms against a sudden gust of wind, but it wasn't cold. The smoky summer wind might have gusted from an oven.

"We got trouble," Luke Ely shouted toward the nearest firefighters.

Sam moved with the men as they fought for a better view of the area where Luke had assigned Nate.

She saw wild horses on the run.

Led by a young bay galloping full out, the horses stampeded down from the hills. What could they be running from? Had wind-borne sparks blown and started a fire they couldn't see from here? Was a fire already burning into the canyon?

When the bay tossed his head, showing a patch of white over one eye, Sam recognized Pirate. Just behind him ran the red roan filly she thought of as Sugar. The horses bumped shoulders and faltered. For a second, the filly veered off course as if the smoke stung her eyes. But then she must have heard the golden-brown mare, trying to keep up, because Sugar's roan legs stretched as she pursued Pirate.

The golden-brown horse was the Phantom's lead mare. Usually, she controlled the herd while the silver stallion watched from above, or hung back where he could see his entire band. But where was he now?

While Sam stood transfixed by the horses' hasty and clumsy descent, Jake and Quinn bolted back toward the other firefighters, who were already hefting the hose. It was then that Sam heard the sound of a cyclone, a tornado, some wild storm rushing their way. Only it wasn't a storm; it was a freakish gale created by the fire.

When Sam turned back to look for the Phantom once more, she could barely see the herd. Dark smoke reduced the mustangs to shadows darting and stumbling in the direction of the captive horses.

Sam squinted and used her hand to shade her eyes, as if that could keep them from tearing up from the smoke.

Something moved, far out in the pasture. Did the wild herd think the other horses were running to safety?

That could be it, Sam decided.

Once, Dark Sunshine had been a decoy, luring other horses into a trap. Sometimes BLM loosed a domestic horse just ahead of wild ones as they fled a hovering helicopter, and they followed the "Judas horse" into a camouflaged corral. Maybe the same thing was happening now.

Pirate reached the pasture fence and raced up and down, looking for a way in. From where she stood, Sam thought he was near the gate, where she'd been painting. What if she ran down and let the wild mustangs into the pasture? Once the horses were confined, the firefighters could protect them.

But if she ran down there, the mustangs would flee. She had to make this decision alone. Jake and the other firefighters were busy. Callie was gone.

Only the fire would help her make this decision.

Red flames danced like tightrope walkers along the top rail of the fence, burning closer and closer to Pirate. He circled away from the fence, looking as if he'd backed up to jump.

She'd heard of fear-maddened horses breaking free of those leading them out of burning barns, to run back to stalls because they were home. But those were domestic horses.

Pirate's determination to run through flames, into the sanctuary pasture, made no sense.

The lead mare wanted to force him back, but clanging metal, the huff from the fire truck's engine, the shouting men, and a dark shroud of smoke turned her trot into a shamble of confusion.

Suddenly a whirlwind of movement swept through the milling herd.

Glinting brightly through the smoke, the Phantom galloped downhill. He ignored the worn path, leaping in sharp turns to make his way through the brush, to take charge of his band.

Read all the Phantom Stallion books!

www.harperteen.com   AVON BOOKS   www.phantomstallion.com
An Imprint of **HarperCollins***Publishers*